Adventure Library

The Forbidden Valley
and other stories

CLIVEDEN PRESS

Contents

THE
FORBIDDEN VALLEY

"Whew! What seamanship!" exclaimed Derek Grant as the tourist boat nosed its way through the rocky approach to Bergen Harbour. His companion, tall, fair-haired Karin Bryant, nodded.

"It gives me a thrill each time I come to Norway," she said.

The two had met on board ship crossing the North Sea. Derek, who intended hiking in Norway and staying at youth hostels, had been grateful for all the advice Karin could give him. It was his first trip abroad, whereas Norway was Karin's second home. Her mother, a Norwegian, had met Karin's father during the war when his plane had crashed on a Norwegian mountain. After their marriage they had lived in England, and now Karin's father was a test pilot; but every summer Karin spent her holiday with her mother's sister in a farm set high in the Norwegian mountains in the shadow of a glacier and an expanse of snowfields.

As the boat docked, Karin remarked, "Now for customs — a mere formality for us."

"Thanks for everything," said Derek. "I hope we meet again. Anyway, I'll take your advice and stay at farms wherever possible."

As they made for the customs-shed a burly, pompous man jostled against Karin, jerking her handbag from her grasp and stepping heavily on her foot. Derek retrieved her bag and glared at the man. Then the glare was wiped off his face. He smiled and said: "I hope you have a good holiday, Mr. Delamore."

The man stopped, and Karin, nursing her aching foot, waited for his apology. But instead he growled rudely, "Didn't know you were coming to Norway, Grant. Keep to the coast. Better for lifts." And, scowling darkly, he went on.

"He's one of the bosses at our lab," murmured Derek. "A super-brain."

"Oh!" said Karin testily. "Manners, however, aren't his strong point. And don't keep to the coast. That's what every tourist does. Go high up the mountains and see real Norwegian life."

"Rather!" promised Derek. And, shaking hands, they parted, Derek to explore the friendly, fascinating town of Bergen, and Karin to board a fiord-steamer that would take her to the isolated hamlet where she would be met by her aunt and her cousins Aase and Giske.

Listening to the lilting Norwegian chatter of her fellow-passengers, Karin felt excited and happy. As the tiny steamer chugged its way through the dark fiord water, turning and twisting into narrow rifts in the lofty cliffs beneath snow and ice, Karin wondered what news her cousins would have for her.

It was late afternoon when the ship's siren blew a shrill blast, the sign that they were approaching a village. Then round a bend appeared the village of Mordal, where Karin would leave the steamer. The small landing-stage was crowded, since the villagers met the steamer which called twice weekly, when the water was free of ice. It was an event which they honoured, whether they had friends on board or not.

Karin soon spotted Aase and Giske in the little crowd. They waved excitedly. Then, on the road leading to the mountains, she saw her aunt seated in the family *stolkjaerre* — a wooden horse-drawn cart-like vehicle used in the mountains. Karin was one of the first to cross the gangway and, having greeted her formally with Scandinavian curtsies, the girls hugged her vigorously.

"Welcome, Karin. Welcome home," said Giske.

"It's been a long year," said Aase.

Seizing her cases, they hurried her to the *stolkjaerre*. She curtsied to her aunt, and then kissed the red, weathered cheek.

"Welcome, child," said her aunt. "My sister, your mother, is well?"

"She is well, and sends her greetings," said Karin as she climbed on to the wooden bench in the back of the *stolkjaerre*.

Her aunt rallied the dozing horse, and, leaving the tiny village, they turned up the mountain road, which rose in hair-raising bends above canyons and a rushing river to the rocky plateau which was the summit.

They were crossing a small stone bridge when a

luxurious car hooted imperiously behind them and, hogging them aside, took the road ahead.

"The English from Olaf Trygusson's *saeter*," said Giske grimly.

"English?" Karin stared, and glimpsed, seated behind the chauffeur, the hateful Mr. Delamore.

"They are not all English," said Aase. "In the village they say that most of the men there are Poles, Czechs and Germans."

"It matters not where they come from," replied Giske crossly. "The valley is forbidden to us. We cannot pick the blueberries and raspberries there this summer."

"That is gossip," said her mother reprovingly. "The gentlemen have rented the valley for the fishing and the hunting this summer. You will be able to pick berries at the mouth of the valley where they are not shooting the reindeer."

"There are only tame reindeer on Olaf's land," argued Giske, "and those are not for hunting. And everybody knows there are no fish in the lake below the glacier."

"And we know it is forbidden to pick the fruit," said Aase. "We . . ." she began, and stopped nervously.

Her mother negotiated an awkward bend successfully. Then she turned to Aase and said, "We will give the horse a rest here, and then you, Aase, can finish what you began saying."

Having pulled into the side of the road, she turned expectantly to her daughters. Karin glanced

at her cousins. They were blushing furiously. So Karin politely studied the view of the distant fiord lying beneath the snow-capped peaks.

Then Giske said: "It was the day you wanted raspberries for jamming, Mother. We went to the good place by the little waterfall at the beginning of Olaf's land, where we've always picked berries. We soon filled our buckets." She stopped, and Aase took up the tale.

"Two men, with a great dog like a wolf, came up to us. One spoke to us in Norwegian, but we were sure that he was not a Norwegian. He asked us who had sent us to spy. I said that nobody had sent us, and that we had always picked the berries in the valley. Then he spoke to the other man in a language we couldn't understand."

Here Giske interrupted, saying, "It was not English. You know, Karin, that we learnt enough English in school to understand even if we cannot speak it well."

Karin nodded worriedly.

"And then?" prompted their mother.

"Then the first man told us to go and not return. The dog growled at us. I think he would have attacked us, but he was on a chain. They took us up to our land," continued Giske, "and watched us leave."

"So," said their mother as she guided the horse back on to the road. "You must keep away from Olaf's land this summer."

As they climbed slowly to the top of the pass

Karin pondered over what her cousins had said. Then she remembered how Mr. Delamore had rudely told Derek to keep away from the mountains. It was all very mysterious.

When they had reached the rocky plateau which topped the steep ascent they could see their house in the distance. It crouched in the shelter of rocks, while above it the grim mountains towered. Around, the peaks glistened with their caps of eternal snow, and between the peaks a glacier thrust its green arms, veined with dark crevasses. The polished log walls of the old house shone in the pale sunshine, and its turf roof was weighed down with slabs of stone against the onslaughts of the great mountain winds. But inside it was snug. Double window-panes kept out the cold, and kept in the heat from the lofty wood-burning stoves that stretched from floor to ceiling in every room. It was a happy house, and as soon as Karin entered she forgot the sinister strangers of the forbidden valley.

The girls helped to prepare the evening meal. Then the outside silence was broken by the tinkling of many bells.

"Father has come with the goats," said Aase, smiling at Karin.

Running outside to greet her uncle, Karin was engulfed by goats. There were white, black and brown goats; nannies and billies, staid old goats and frisky kids. Her uncle had brought them down from their scanty pastures to be milked and fed.

The following days were typical of life in the summer in the Norwegian mountains. The girls helped with the household chores. They picked the wild berries for jam, and milked the goats morning and evening.

One sunny evening, as the two girls were diligently milking the goats, Giske said suddenly: "Look! Father's coming with a stranger."

Aase and Karin straightened their backs and turned to stare.

"Whoever it is, he's lame, and Father's carrying his rucksack," said Aase.

Suddenly Karin exclaimed: "Why! I know him! It's Derek Grant. We met on the boat coming from England."

"Go quickly," said Giske. "We will finish the milking."

As Karin ran towards the house, which Derek and her uncle had entered, she grinned as she remembered how she had told Derek to make for the mountains. He'd evidently taken her advice, and got into trouble. Then it struck her that her uncle and Derek had come from the direction of the forbidden valley. Had Derek been seeking Mr. Delamore?

Entering the kitchen, she was amused to see Derek seated at the table with a cup of neglected coffee before him, while he, frowning heavily, thumbed his way through a phrase-book. Derek was evidently having language difficulties.

"Can I help you?" asked Karin primly. Control-

ling her giggles, she thought she sounded exactly like a well-trained English shop assistant.

"English!" exclaimed Derek thankfully. Then he looked up, and, seeing Karin, said, "What a break! Am I glad to see you!"

He tried to stand, and winced.

"What's wrong with your foot?" asked Karin.

"Sprained my ankle on the mountains. It's lucky that this gentleman, who must be your uncle, saw me limping along. How far am I from a youth hostel?"

Turning to her uncle and aunt, Karin explained that she knew Derek and that he wanted to go on to a youth hostel.

"Nonsense!" said her uncle. "See to his foot, Karin. He has a small tent, so he must camp here until his foot is right. Youth hostel indeed!"

Later, when she had bandaged his foot and he was eating a hot meal, Karin asked Derek, "Were you trying to get to your friend Mr. Delamore?"

"Delamore? Is he up here? And he's not my friend. He's one of my bosses. A mere dogsbody like me wouldn't dare seek out Delamore outside lab routine work."

Then he became serious.

"Apparently," he said, "I trespassed this afternoon. I thought the mountains were free for all, and I wanted to get up near the glacier. I meant to camp there tonight."

"Yes," prompted Karin gently.

"I was getting along quite nicely, when suddenly

a mighty big alsatian swooped on me, and got me to the ground." Derek grinned sheepishly. "In fact I thought I'd been attacked by a wolf."

"And then?" asked Karin, leaning forward.

"Two men came and called off the wolf, I mean dog, and began gabbling in what I vow was German. I don't speak German, but once I worked with a German refugee, who used to talk to himself when an experiment went wrong. These men sounded just like old Hans in a rage."

"Didn't you try to explain?" asked Karin.

"I told them 'English'. Then one told me in broken English, 'Go. Mountain forbidden.' So I scrammed, and fell on some scree."

Sighing, Karin told him how some visitors supposed to be English, had taken the valley for the hunting and fishing.

"And Delamore is there?" asked Derek incredulously.

Karin nodded.

"He may fish, though I doubt it," said Derek thoughtfully. "But he certainly can't shoot. I remember him saying so when on a firm's outing we went to a showground shooting-booth for a lark."

"Perhaps he's wearing L for Learner," grinned Karin.

But Derek was serious. At last he said slowly, "You've made me curious, Karin. I think I'm going to drop in on that valley again. Delamore isn't the type to go in for fun and games."

"You won't be able to go anywhere for a week

or so, with that ankle," remarked Karin.

"No. But when I am mobile again, are you game to come with me? You know the lay of the land."

There was a moment's silence broken only by the plaintive bleating of the goats outside. Then, nodding briskly, Karin said, "I'll come. And I've just remembered there's another little-known entrance to that valley. I'll tell you later. But not a word to my family. My aunt would forbid it. And say nothing in front of the girls — they understand English. I don't want to get them into trouble with their mother."

For the best part of a week Derek nursed his crocked ankle. One day, as they sat outside his tent with their backs against a boulder, Derek said suddenly, "Pretty rocky that valley of Delamore's isn't it?"

Karin grinned.

"This part of Norway," she replied, "is mostly rock — where it isn't fiord, mountain lakes, and ice and snow. It's a relic of the Ice Age."

"Yes. That Ice Age. Very old, and very modern too," said Derek pensively.

"You speak in riddles, friend," said Karin lazily.

Then a humming noise overhead brought her to her feet.

"A helicopter!" she exclaimed. "I've never seen one here before."

With narrowed eyes Derek watched the machine. Then he sat up, saying, "Isn't it heading in the direction of Delamore's valley?"

"Yes."

Derek got up carefully. Testing his foot, he said:

"I think my foot could do with some exercise now. Let's go down to the fiord-village tomorrow. If my ankle stands up to the walk there and back I'll be able to do our jaunt into the valley."

Karin frowned. "Why rush things?" she asked.

"Because the time-factor is chancy; and we don't know how long the key men will stay up there," said Derek, more to himself than to Karin.

"Time factor? Key men?" asked Karin bewildered.

"I may be wrong, Karin. But Delamore's presence is giving me ideas. That little company in the valley may be on to something that's important, and dangerous in the wrong hands."

"You've been reading too many thrillers," scoffed Karin. "I loathe the man, but what harm can he do in an isolated Norwegian valley?"

Shrugging his shoulders Derek said, "Forget it. But promise to guide me in, please."

"I have promised, and I'm just as inquisitive as you are."

The following day the two set out for the village on the fiord. After a little stiffness Derek said that his ankle improved with every step. Once in the village they made for the village shop which was also the post office, as the sign with the postman's horn above the door showed. To Karin's surprise the chauffeur who had driven Delamore up the pass was collecting mail and speaking to the postmistress in German. She curtly handed him a bundle of letters, and when he had gone said to Karin, "I cannot be polite to Germans. You know, Karin, my Nils died at their hands in the Resistance."

Karin nodded gently. Then she said: "He's from Olaf's valley, isn't he?"

"Yes. There are all kinds up there — English, Poles, Czechs, Germans, and maybe Russians."

"Are there many English up there?" asked Karin.

"Only the one who rented the land from Olaf," was the reply. "He wrote from London. He must be rich, because they have a helicopter and a seaplane which lands on the lake by the glacier."

On the homeward climb Karin and Derek discussed the situation. Derek was anxious to leave for the valley early next morning, while the mist still covered the mountains, and so their movements would be less easily seen.

"Could you find the way in thick mist?" he asked.

"It would be tricky," replied Karin. "But I know the danger spots. But a better idea would be to leave my aunt's late in the afternoon, and stay the night in the refuge hut which is near the secret entrance to the valley. Then we would be fresh and more alert if we meet trouble."

"How secret is this way in? And do you think it will be patrolled?"

"I'm sure it will not be guarded because they wouldn't expect intruders from that direction. And it is really secret. Only the real mountain people know of it. It's a kind of ladder."

"Ladder?" exclaimed Derek.

Karin laughed at his dismayed expression.

"Not a wooden affair, but a series of steps hewn in the rock-walls countless years ago, before a road into the valley was ever dreamt of. It's difficult, and could be dangerous. But I'd rather risk a track I know than meet a ferocious dog that I don't."

"There's something to be said for that argument," grinned Derek. "I don't fancy being pawed and smelt by that beast again."

"A climb in the mountains will do you good, Karin," said her aunt next day as she packed two rucksacks with provisions for Karin and Derek.

"I hope aunt's right," muttered Karin to Derek. She felt excited and also scared at the adventurous prospect ahead of them. In addition to his rucksack, Derek carried a climbing-rope wound round his middle. This was Karin's idea.

They began their adventure in bright sunshine. Excitedly they climbed steadily, passing through moorland bestrewn with boulders and ice-green lakes; then they passed through a rocky canyon. Finally they reached a wilderness of bare rock with expanses of last year's snow in its hollows. Above, mountains of sheer rock with their peaks capped with snow encircled them, and within walking distance a glacier thrust its green arm menacingly towards them.

They had been silent for a long time. Then as Derek stared in dismay at the pathless desert of rock, Karin whispered as if afraid to break the silence: "There's the hut."

The refuge was anchored to boulders with strong wire cables, and its roof held down by huge slabs of stone. Derek followed Karin towards it. It consisted of two small rooms with four bunks in each. One room had a huge cast-iron stove laid with logs ready for lighting.

"Get snow in this pan while I get the fire going," said Karin. "Then I'll make the cocoa."

The warmth from the log fire and a meal of cocoa, sardines and crispbread followed by fruit, relaxed and refreshed them. Then, sitting in the glow from the fire, they discussed their plans for the morrow.

"We must leave about four in the morning," said Karin, "when the thick mist will give us good cover."

"Tell me more about this ladder," suggested Derek. "You've actually used it?"

"I've been down it twice with my uncle," said Karin. "I'll go first. You'd better rope me to you in case I slip. There are twenty-seven steps, and some may be slippery. So the going will be slow."

"I can't help thinking of that dog," Derek remarked uneasily.

"I should think it will be chained up at that hour," comforted Karin. "Anyway the dogs are probably used to guard the lower entrance where a regular path enters the valley. However, if we're caught we must say that we're lost."

"Too true," grinned Derek. "We'll be lost all right if we're caught."

"When we reach the bottom of the ladder," continued Karin, "we go right, towards the *saeter*. After that it will depend on what we see. What do you expect to see, Derek?"

Derek shrugged. "Men at work," he said, "and not good old English workmen, either. What about the road back?"

"I hope to pick up a path between the lake and the glacier. It's roundabout, but it leads eventually to the ladder."

Bolting the door, they took turns to sleep two hours at a time, so that they would be sure of an early start.

After a hasty breakfast they got ready. They were travelling light, taking only the rope, some chocolate, raisins, and an apple apiece in their pockets. Derek gazed longingly at some goat-cheese and crispbread that Karin replaced in her rucksack.

"No," she said firmly. "There'll be plenty of good water and wild berries."

Derek grimaced. "No diet for a growing boy," he teased.

"Come along," said Karin severely.

They slipped out of the hut, and walked in single file with Karin leading, into a blanket of mist. A cold wind blew off the glacier, and both were glad of the anoraks with hoods they had borrowed from Aase and Giske.

Visibility extended only a couple of feet ahead, and their progress was slow. Suddenly Karin stopped at what seemed to Derek to be a bottomless cauldron of mist.

"Rope," she whispered.

Deftly Derek roped them together, grateful for the training he'd had on an Outward Bound course.

"Here we go," muttered Karin. "I wish us luck!"

Derek smiled bleakly.

Intent on their descent, they had no time for fear. Both mentally counted the steps, and both sighed with relief when they reached the twenty-seventh. Some steps had been slippery, and Karin, who knew the depth of the rugged drop below them, had several uneasy moments.

As they rested at the foot of the stone ladder Derek suddenly saw a light flicker nearby. Gripping Karin's arm, he pointed. The light shone palely in the mist.

"House," whispered Karin. "Come on. Hold my coat."

Slowly they walked through heather. Then they heard the soft lapping of water, and Derek knew without being told that they were near the glacier's lake. They were almost upon the light when Karin stopped abruptly, and crawled on all fours into a rocky hide-out, pulling Derek after her. This natural rocky refuge had only one opening, and this gave an excellent view of the light. The mist was thinning, and Derek could see the outlines of two buildings.

Suddenly the mist lifted, and the farm-house door opened. Two men with a dog on a chain came out. Karin felt Derek stiffen. Fortunately the wind carried their scent away from the animal, and the men led him down towards the lower entrance of the valley. Karin smiled, and Derek gave a thumbs-up sign.

Shortly afterwards two other men came out carrying equipment. Derek narrowed his eyes, and nudged Karin violently. Moving clumsily with their burdens these men climbed the rocks above the lake towards the glacier.

Putting his mouth to Karin's ear, Derek asked, "Can we stalk them?"

Karin hesitated, scanning the landscape. Then nodding, she slipped out, and ran noiselessly on the blueberry plants, flitting from boulder to boulder. Derek followed her closely. The strangers were now ploughing their way over scree below the glacier. Karin and Derek realised that they could not attempt to stalk them any farther because there was no cover, and the small flints clattering beneath their feet would betray their presence. So, huddled beneath a rock, they waited and watched. A tinkling noise puzzled Karin. She turned to Derek with lifted eyebrows.

"Geologists hammering for specimens," he whispered against her ear, "I've seen enough. Let's go."

Karin shook her head. "Can't. They're in our way!"

At that moment a throbbing noise surged up the valley. It was followed by a seaplane, which in a matter of seconds landed on the lake. So intent were Derek and Karin on this that they forgot the geologists until they heard them clatter down the scree towards the lake. They were soon joined by more men from the buildings, among them Delamore. When they were all engrossed with the occupants of the seaplane Karin tugged Derek's arm, and whispered, "Quick!"

They dashed from cover to cover to reach the paths around the glacier, known only to reindeer and Norwegians.

It was a nightmare flight, and both were breathless when Karin stopped, and sinking on to a rock panted, "We're safe."

For a few minutes neither spoke. Then Karin asked quietly, "What do they expect to find in their rock specimens – gold?"
f the man's signals and promised him a good tip if he would take the three of them to the Rue Blanc.

Grimly Derek said, "No. My guess is uranium. And since there isn't a Norwegian amongst them, I think they mean to smuggle their finds out. To what country? Your guess is as good as mine."

"But that's stealing," gasped Karin.

Derek nodded. "And Delamore is a traitor. Let's get out. Where's our ladder?"

Karin was thoughtful as she led the way to their rocky staircase. They had reached its foot when, with a menacing throb, a helicopter hovered above them. Instinctively they both hid their faces and flattened themselves against the rock-face. But though the machine disappeared the way it had come, and was evidently off route, they both knew they had been seen.

Derek looked at Karin's white face.

"At least," he said, "they can't land here. The rocks are too close."

Mechanically they climbed up the stone steps. Once at the top they hid again in a circle of boulders. Then, deciding all was well, they came out into the open. Immediately, with its sinister hum, the helicopter returned. Petrified, they stared at it, and at the man descending from it. Then they saw that he carried a gun.

There seemed no escape. Still, Derek yelled, "Run. Dodge."

For a second Karin seemed stunned. Then in a low voice she said, "Follow me. Wherever I go."

Then she ran, zigzagging between boulders towards the ladder. But instead of going down, she swerved left where the rocks were close together. Half conscious of a mighty roar, Derek followed her. Round a bend they came up against an immense three-armed waterfall.

Over her shoulder Karin asked, "Can you see him?"

Derek looked behind carefully, and gasped, "Not in sight."

Karin looked up at the empty sky. They seemed safe from spying eyes.

"Now follow," she panted, and plunged straight at the middle waterfall. For a split second Derek hesitated. This seemed madness. Then he too ran into the fall. To his surprise he found himself in a small cave. Hidden under the middle fall was a protruding rock, so it was possible to dash under it, and enter the cave without getting wet.

Inside the cave the outside light filtered greenly through the water. Talking was impossible because of the roar of the three torrents. Standing beneath their curtain of water they waited for their pursuers. Their wait was short. Two men, both armed, came along the track, to be brought up sharply by the impassable cataracts. They searched every available cranny, then, shrugging their shoulders and shaking their heads, they turned back. One pointed significantly towards the canyon below. He evidently thought that Karin and Derek had fallen into the forbidden valley down below.

Shaking with reaction and the creeping cold, Karin rubbed some warmth into her limbs. Derek produced his packet of raisins, and then a bar of chocolate. But the cold mountain water cupped in their hands was more refreshing than either. They became stiff and cold, so they marched solemnly up and down, and round and round their tiny refuge.

It was not until nightfall that they felt it was safe to leave. Once outside, Karin tugged at the rope round Derek's waist. He understood, and roped them together again. Then, climbing over stunted shrubs, they gained a path that wound up and

above the waterfalls. It was rough going, and in places they had to crawl on all fours.

Suddenly a great silence hit Derek's ears. Then he realised that they had left the waterfalls far behind.

"Hello, pal," said Karin hoarsely. "A rest and chocolate, I think."

Gratefully they sat down under a sky brilliant with stars, and munched happily.

"Where are we?" asked Derek at last.

"On the mountain below the glacier which faces our house. In distance we haven't far to go, but we must skirt a snowfield, testing every step as we go. One slip would mean cold storage for keeps!"

"You've been a grand leader," said Derek self-consciously.

"It was pleasanter doing it by daylight with Uncle," confessed Karin. "But anything is better than playing hide-and-seek with that helicopter. Let's get moving."

Neither would ever forget the rest of the journey. Several times Karin stumbled, and once she fell into a snow-hole, to be hauled out quickly by Derek.

At last they came to a rough path.

"The worst is over," said Karin gaily. "We're on a goat-track that leads directly home."

"What's that light?" asked Derek. "There! Oh, it's hidden by a bend. There it is again."

Karin giggled hysterically.

"Now, we've had everything! It's a search-party."

Now, though bone-weary, the whole adventure seemed to have been fun. Cheerfully they yodelled to their friends below. But Karin had another surprise when the two parties met.

A tall, slim man stepped forward in front of her uncle and her cousins.

"Daddy!" yelled Karin. "Gosh! Who sent for you?"

"Nobody, Puss," he replied. "I was testing a new plane, and thought I'd join you."

Introducing Derek, Karin said, "And Daddy'll know what to do about Delamore and company."

"We had better get home," said Giske. "Mother has worried. She feared that Derek's foot was poor again."

So it was over an immense hot meal that they told their tale, with Giske, helped by Aase, translating quickly for their parents.

Karin's father listened intently.

"You are sure of your facts?" he asked Derek.

"Sure!" spluttered Karin. "If you think we dreamt up those geologists, and that beastly helicopter, and those gangsters with guns!"

Meanwhile, Derek, grinning at Karin's outburst, managed to nod to her father.

"Fair enough! I know a chap in Oslo who'll know what to do."

So that afternoon security forces closed in by land and air on the forbidden valley. And since spies can claim no protection from their masters, the fate of the men who had rented Olaf Trygusson's land created no diplomatic situation.

Later, Derek returned to his lab work, but Mr. Delamore did not. It would be a long time before he would be free to leave an English prison.

33

THE TOYSHOP MYSTERY

"It's snowing," said Sally Baxter delightedly, looking out of the office window into Fleet Street, where the early-morning traffic was making its way through a flurry of white. "Isn't that marvellous? The country will look lovely. It may even be cold enough to skate."

"By which I presume you have got a Christmas holiday while the rest of us slog away on duty? Ah well; we can't all be beautiful brunettes."

She grinned at the other junior reporter, who was leaning with an elbow on his typewriter in an attitude supposed to register despair.

"Come off it, Ian. I know perfectly well you are having your break at New Year so that you can go back to Scotland," she said. "And you don't intend to work particularly hard for the *Evening Cry* between now and then. Just one party after another while I go out on this perfectly awful assignment for the 'People who work at Christmas' series. The news editor has let you off while I. . . ."

"Let me guess. Deliver mail? Or sweep the streets?"

"Nearly as bad. Sell toys at Marshaws."

"So that's why you are wearing your little black frock?" the boy teased. "I thought you had joined the canteen staff."

Sally glanced at her watch and began to gather up her notebook and pen. As one of the few teenage reporters in the national newpaper office she was used to being teased, and even the note of jealousy in Ian's voice when he talked of a Christmas holiday did not worry her.

Although no newspapers were published on Christmas Day, there always had to be a skeleton staff on duty in Fleet Street and for the past three years she had been among the unlucky ones who had worked. This time, however, she was to finish early on December 24th and travel down to join her mother in the country at Nashbridge.

But before then she had a job to do. Don Howe, the news editor, had scattered his staff round the country doing the work that the Christmas rush entailed.

"You will go to that snooty store in the West End and sell toys, Sally," he had decided. "Write a human story about what it feels like to be a salesgirl. Aching back, tired feet. . . . You know the kind of stuff I want."

He had never spoken truer words, thought Sally later that day as, bewildered and flushed, she tried to master the art of selling teddy bears and dolls to the hundreds of harassed mothers and fathers who milled round her.

The other members of the sales staff had tried to tell her as much about the job as they could, but time was short. It was just a question of keeping her head and her temper as she struggled to wrap up parcels which just refused to come up to the Marshaw standard.

"I never was much good at mental arithmetic," she muttered to herself as she dashed over towards a till. "How much is £9.50, £6.99 and 15p! I am sure I could have done it if that child hadn't insisted on wanting a 15p balloon as well as a doll and a cot."

"£16.64," said a quiet voice by her side, and after Sally had handed over the parcels and the change she stopped by the side of a girl who sat at a desk, recording some figures in a book.

"Thank you. I keep getting into a flap. Never worked so hard in my life," she panted. "Perhaps I could break off now and go for some lunch. I wish I could look as calm as you do instead of getting hot dashing round the counters."

"And I wish I could dash around," the girl answered, with a sudden smile which brought a blush to Sally's cheeks. She had not noticed until that moment that one of her new friend's legs was held stiffly in front of her, with an iron brace clamped round it.

"I'm sorry," she said quickly. "I hadn't a clue. . . . Was it polio?"

"Yes, but I am used to it. Marshaws are very good. They have given me this sitting-down job numbering the parcels. You see, that is my grandfather over there."

Sally looked across the desk and spotted a familiar, white-whiskered figure.

"Santa Claus! Why, I have been too busy to notice him. There's been such a crowd in this corner I could not see what was going on."

The lame girl's eyes twinkled. "He has a 'post office' there. After people have bought toys the parcels are weighed and I write names and addresses on them. The parents pay the cost of the postage, and then the children 'post' them in Father Christmas's sack. It's a tremendous thrill for them because, of course, they are all delivered to their friends by reindeer."

"I would have loved it myself," Sally confessed. "Well, the crowds have certainly thinned off now so I will report to the supervisor and see if I can get some lunch. I want to write down some of my impressions before I pass out completely."

By the end of the afternoon Sally found that she was getting the hang of the job and began to enjoy herself as she bent down to catch the whispered requests made to her by children or tried to find exactly the right toy for some of the rich customers whose families appeared to have everything they wanted.

Occasionally she found time to check some of her calculations with Mary Inman, the lame girl, and to spend a minute or two watching the children 'posting' their parcels in Father Christmas's sack. She was relieved to know that the packages would be re-wrapped before they went to the real post office, otherwise some of her own bundles, she thought, would never reach their destination.

By the end of the day, after she had gathered some facts and figures to add to her article, she was weary.

The giant luxury store had closed its doors for the night and the tired assistants were streaming out of the staff doorway into the snow.

One by one they punched the time-clock, said goodnight to the doorman, and disappeared. For the first time Sally realised what the Christmas rush really meant for those who had to work in a shop and she felt she would write a glowing article about them which would touch the hearts of the *Evening Cry*'s readers.

In front of her she could see Mary Inman limping slowly down the corridor with her grandfather who, now stripped of his scarlet robes and beard, looked a fragile old man.

Thinking she would like to say goodbye and thank the girl again for her help, she hurried to join them. But a sudden burst of angry shouting from the doorman, who had been joined by two of his colleagues, stopped her.

To her dismay she realised that something was wrong. The sack which the children had filled and re-filled during the day with their parcels lay on the floor. In the doorman's hand was a small brown-paper parcel, which he had ripped open and was brandishing towards the old man.

Two men in lounge suits joined the group and Sally could see that deep distress was written on the faces of Mary and her grandfather.

With her reporter's instincts aroused, she went forward to join the group. Mary turned to her, tears streaming down her white cheeks.

"What on earth has happened?" she asked the stricken girl. "Is your grandfather in trouble?"

Everyone seemed to be speaking at once, but eventually one of the supervisors turned to Sally, with a fastidious shudder.

"I am sorry you have seen this, Miss Baxter," he said agitatedly. "Of course, these things never happen with our regular staff but when we have temporary workers there are isolated cases of theft. This man, our Father Christmas, came to us with the highest references but the doorman spotted him carrying his sack out of the building, rolled up under his arm. Just as a precaution he took it off him and shook it. This parcel fell out — and you will see what it contains. A dozen very expensive gold wrist-watches."

"But I didn't know it was in the sack. I had no idea. . . . I know nothing about it."

Sally's heart was touched by the absolute sincerity in the old man's voice.

"Why were you taking the sack home?" she asked gently, and Mary replied.

"There was a tear in it . . . and grandfather thought my mother would sew it up so it would be all right for tomorrow. She is a dressmaker. We are not thieves."

There was dignity in the girl's voice and even the irate supervisors seemed impressed.

Sally felt a quick urge to do something to help.

"You can't solve this problem tonight. Mr Inman is very tired and shaken. Can't you just keep the watches and sort the whole thing out tomorrow? I am sure there must be some explanation."

The head supervisor wavered.

"Well, of course, we should not like to read anything in the *Evening Cry* about this. Marshaws never get their name in the paper that way . . . and we are all anxious to get home before it starts snowing again."

"Then let's call it a day," said Sally briskly, feeling that the situation was going her way. "I have my car on the staff parking ground. I'll run the Inmans home and you can start your questioning again tomorrow."

The car was new and the girl reporter felt that she would never again use it for a sadder errand. The girl was quietly sobbing and old Tom Inman seemed stunned by the accusation that had been brought against him.

"I thought the sack was empty," he moaned. "All the parcels the children posted had been emptied out and their numbers corresponded with the check Mary had made in her book. I don't know where those watches came from . . . I really don't know."

Sally was convinced she could believe him, and when she sat in the tidy little sitting-room at the Inmans' home, she sensed that she was among good people.

"You see, my mother is a dressmaker," said Mary quietly, as she limped across the room to uncover an electric machine. "Ever since I was ill she has taken in sewing to help to keep us. My father died two years ago, and the three of us live together."

After Mrs Inman, who seemed as stunned as her father-in-law at the bad news, had made a cup of tea, Sally tried to collect her thoughts, although her head was spinning with fatigue.

"Now, let's think how the parcel of watches could have got into your sack," she said practically. "It was very small. Could one of the children have 'posted' it by mistake, do you think?"

"It wasn't addressed," broke in Mary. "So it didn't go through the same drill as all the other packages."

Sally leaned forward quickly. "Were all the parcels put into your sack by children?" she asked the old man. "Do you remember any grown-up 'posting' that packet?"

Tom Inman's eyes brightened. "There was one woman, just before closing-time. She put something into my sack and I asked her if she had had it weighed and addressed. She said something to me in a sort of foreign voice. I couldn't understand what she said. The next minute she was lost in the crowd and there were so many children clamouring for their turn, I never gave it another thought."

"What did she look like?" asked Sally, urgently.

He could hardly remember, Father Christmas told her, but had got the impression that she was tall and dressed in a short fur jacket and a light skirt.

"She wore one of those bracelets with a lot of odds and ends dangling from it. I remember that because it caught in the top of the sack and she snatched her hand away quickly as though she was angry about it."

Sally drove back to her lodgings very slowly, through the slushy streets. She knew she had left sorrow behind her at Christmas-time and was determined to try her best to cure it.

She would not be able to enjoy her own holiday if the thought of sadness at the Inmans' home was nagging in her mind.

Although she would gladly have crawled into bed after having her bath Sally had to sit down at her typewriter to create the article needed for the next day's *Evening Cry* about her experiences as a toy salesgirl at Marshaws' exclusive store.

It was not difficult to write, for, she thought ruefully, she still had the headache, backache and footache the strenuous day had given her. But she had not expected to have heartache as well, yet that was what she was experiencing, as the thought of Mary Inman's tear-stained face and the trembling hands of the old man kept coming back to her.

Tom Inman had taken such a pride in his job, she remembered. He loved children and knew just how to talk to them in the role of Father Christmas. To feel that even at the age of seventy he could get work, Mrs Inman had told her, made him happy, but now, despairing and suspected of theft, or collusion with a store thief, he was a broken man.

She glanced at the calendar. December 22nd. There was only one more working day before she could put the cover on her typewriter and travel to Nashbridge to start her Christmas break. Could she possibly do anything, in that one day, to help the Inmans?

Acting on impulse, she picked up the telephone and gave the Fleet Street number. Instead of taking her article to the office the next morning, she would dictate it to one of the typists who was on duty all night.

The man typed the words she read out as quickly as she could speak. At the end she asked him to leave a message for the chief reporter.

"Am returning to Marshaws in the morning instead of coming into the office. Story broke just as I was leaving which I want to follow up," she dictated. Then she went to bed feeling a little easier in her mind.

The people at Marshaws seemed surprised to see her before opening-time, for she had arranged to work on the staff for only one day. She explained that she had not come to sell toys but to absorb a little more atmosphere and see if there was any news about the watches.

On the surface, everything looked just the same as on the previous day. Father Christmas was settling in his corner with his sack, and a girl was waiting to address the parcels for the little children to 'post'. But both were new store assistants hurriedly transferred to take the place of Tom and Mary, who had been dismissed on suspicion.

Sally was soon hard at work on her investigations. In a departmental manager's office she learned that the store detectives were puzzled about the mysterious parcel of watches.

"We came in very early this morning and checked our stock of that particular make of Swiss watch. As far as we can see, none is missing from the jewellery department," confessed the head detective.

"Then Tom Inman did not steal them from you," Sally said quickly. "Surely that clears him and he can return to his job?"

"It partly clears him, but we cannot overlook the fact that he was taking valuables off the premises in one of the firm's sacks," said the manager in an outraged voice. "The whole thing is highly suspicious. What was he doing with the watches, we should like to know? Until he confesses we cannot have him on our staff, or his granddaughter either."

Sally sighed. "Have you been to the police?"

The men exchanged glances and the manager cleared his throat.

"No . . . not yet. Perhaps after the Christmas rush we shall have to report the facts, but you know, Sally, Marshaws have a very high reputation. We try to avoid any scandal if at all poss-ible. As the watches do not appear to be our pro-perty, we shall keep them in a safe place for a few days to see if there are any inquiries."

"And in the meantime the Inmans will have a miserable Christmas unless I can do something about it," Sally thought as she wandered back into the store, which had just opened its doors to the public. She stood watching the first customers coming out of the lift on the toy floor, a stream of determined shoppers wanting to miss the rush which would come later.

Suddenly her heart beat a little faster. Crossing the floor towards Father Christmas was a tall woman in a short mink jacket over a beige frock. Her sallow face and brown eyes seemed anxious as she paused by the red-cloaked figure.

The new Father Christmas looked nothing like the one who had been on duty the day before.

Tom Inman was a slightly built, small man with twinkling blue eyes. The man who had taken his place was much taller, with a hooked nose and dark eyes.

Sally walked over to stand beside the woman and she drew a sharp breath as she saw a bracelet heavy with gold charms jangle on her wrist. This was the stranger Mr Inman had described the night before.

She was speaking now, in broken English, to Father Christmas, who was bending to catch her words.

"I have only just come on duty, madam," he said. "The man who was acting as Santa Claus yesterday is not here today."

Sally felt delighted that the woman seemed disturbed at the news and was glancing over her shoulder rather wildly as though she were looking out for someone.

Being a reporter on a national newspaper had often meant playing amateur detective. The girl had to think quickly of some way she could identify the woman and link her with the parcel of watches.

But before she had time to make a plan, something happened with dramatic suddenness.

The woman, who was already pale, had gone deathly white and her eyes glanced round the store as if she wanted a way of escape. She muttered something under her breath.

Sally, watching keenly, realised in a flash what had caused the mink-coated figure to panic. A swarthy man, with dark glasses, wearing a heavy waterproof, had come into the toy department and was making his way through the crowd of shoppers towards them.

Her reporter's instinct told her the woman wanted to get out of his way.

Quickly she turned to the stranger and in a low voice said, "Do you want to leave the store, madam? If you will come with me I will take you to the lift."

The gloved hand, with its jingling bracelet, clutched her arm.

"*Merci.* I feel faint. . . . I must get into the open air."

Sally pushed her roughly through a door marked "Private", which she remembered from the previous day led into a corridor used by the staff.

The service lift, luckily, was standing un-attended, and in a second she and the woman she judged to be French, or French-speaking Swiss, were descending to street-level at the back of the building.

The woman leant against the wall saying nothing, but showing signs of agitation. She closed her eyes, only opening them when the lift came to a halt.

"This way," said Sally, walking towards the staff exit, where she explained to the doorman that a customer felt ill and wanted to go out.

"I'll get you a taxi. There is one on the rank at the street corner," said the man, putting his finger in his mouth and giving a shrill whistle. When they were inside the cab, with the woman still looking anxiously around to see if she were being followed, Sally asked where she wanted to go.

"The airport. Quickly."

The words gave the girl a shock, but her reaction was quick.

"What a coincidence, madame. I am going there myself. I was just killing time in the store," she said. "My plane leaves before lunch."

"To Paris?" the woman said nervously. "That is lucky, for we can share the taxi. I am very fortunate to have met you. You are going to France for Christmas?"

"No. Just on a business trip, returning almost immediately," improvised Sally, realising she had no luggage to back up her story and hoping her handbag looked bulky enough to contain her night things. But the woman was too worried to notice details, and when the taxi reached the airport she clung to Sally as though she wanted moral support as they went into the reception lounge.

The stranger, once inside, seemed anxious to lose her, but Sally was determined to ignore her wishes. "Let's have coffee," she said briefly, leading the way to a table.

The woman looked across the lounge and said abruptly, "Do you speak French well?"

"I wish I did. No, English is my language," Sally answered, thankful that she did not have to tell a deliberate lie as her French was, in fact, quite fluent, a fact she obviously was not prepared to let the suspected crook know.

Seeming satisfied, the woman sat down and beckoned to someone across the lounge. Immediately a man, obviously also a foreigner, joined them and, without making an introduction, her companion spoke to him in French.

"It is all right. We can speak freely. She only understands English. I cannot get rid of her because she helped me to escape from Marshaws — and Jacques."

The man drew a quick breath and dropped his

voice to a whisper. Sally, trying to make her face a blank, listened as intently as she could, but the clatter of the lounge, with flight announcements being made every minute or so over the airport loud-speaker system, made it hard for her to catch more than an odd word now and then.

There was talk of a "package", a word which made her ears prick, and frequent references to "Jacques", whom they both seemed to fear. When it was evident that the couple were taking the 11.15 plane to Paris, Sally knew she must work fast.

Excusing herself, she hurried to the ticket office, where she was relieved to find a man on duty whom she knew from many other flights for *Evening Cry* assignments.

"Mike, I need your help. I must get the 11.15 plane to Paris," she told him.

"You'll be lucky. We are in the middle of the Christmas rush. There isn't a seat vacant. Come back in the New Year," he replied with a grin.

"This is important. I am after a scoop which might save a nice old man and a girl with polio from having a desperately unhappy Christmas. Please help me. I am sure you must have just one seat up your sleeve I could book."

He sighed, picked up some papers, and then brightened.

"There's a relief plane at 11.45, with a cancellation. How about that?"

"I'm sorry, but it must be the earlier plane. Can't you transfer someone to give me a chance?"

"I suppose so, seeing you are a V.I.P. in the newspaper world. Have you got any money? Not much? Well, we'll charge it to the *Cry* as usual. Passport? Good girl; I know you always carry it in that bulging handbag of yours. Right. You can take a seat on the 11.15. Good luck, Sally."

The man and woman she was stalking greeted her coldly as they entered the plane and she got as near to them as she could.

As the aircraft took off she rubbed her forehead dazedly, realising just what she had done. It was now December 23rd and the next morning she ought to have been taking a train for a Christmas holiday in the countryside of rural England. Instead, she was on a plane flying to France, with no luggage and not much money. No-one, apart from the booking clerk, knew where she was at that moment and yet she was coolly getting entangled with a pair of strangers she suspected to be crooks.

Had the woman made a genuine mistake in 'posting' the parcel in the sack? If so, her own trip to Paris was unnecessary and would need some explaining away at the office.

Quickly Sally dismissed the thought. Anyone who had made a mistake would have asked to see the manager of the store, but the fur-coated stranger had acted furtively, obviously terrified at the appearance of "Jacques" in the toy department.

Sally gazed down at the snowy fields below her and then at the English Channel which looked grey and cold through the clouds. What would her mother say if she knew her daughter, for whom she would be making such happy preparations, was off on another adventure so near to Christmas Eve? Still, the life of a reporter was like that, and Mrs Baxter had learned to keep calm when other mothers would be in a state of panic.

She came out of her day-dream when she heard the woman's voice say, "Can we return the compliment, mademoiselle, and offer you a lift in our taxi, when we get to Paris?"

"That depends where you are going," she answered quickly, and congratulated herself when the stranger said, "The Rue Blanc. It is near the Opéra."

"That would do splendidly. I would be glad of a lift."

Just what her own plans were she did not know, but she was determined not to lose sight of the pair. If she could see where they lived or were staying, she would be one step nearer in her investigations.

But luck was against her. Icy conditions delayed the landing and the Christmas bustle at the airport caught them in a tangle of traffic. It was then, trying to secure a taxi, that Sally made her first mistake.

Instinctively she broke into her best French as she tried to speed up the process. She clutched hold of a reluctant taxi-driver who had taken no notice of the man's signals and promised him a good tip if he would take the three of them to the Rue Blanc.

When she turned in triumph towards the others she found they were looking at her in horror.

"So you do speak French," said the woman furiously. "What is this? A plot to trap us?"

Things happened quickly then. The man, with a grunt, gave Sally a sharp push with his hand and sent her sprawling on to the ground. She leapt up as quickly as she could, but it was too late. The couple had entered the taxi, which was being driven rapidly away as she stood, scarlet-faced, knowing she had blundered.

The noise around her was bewildering. The relief plane had already arrived from England and the crowd wanting taxis was larger than ever. Sally realised that she must change some English money into French francs, and it was quite a time before she eventually got a taxi for herself, giving the address the couple had told her was their destination.

The man drove slowly for a Frenchman, as the roads were slippery with ice, and snow was again falling from the grey sky.

Suddenly he looked in his driving-mirror and said, "Mademoiselle, have you a friend seeking you? We are being followed, and the man inside the cab is signalling that he wants us to stop."

Sally, shivering with cold and a nameless fear, looked behind. Leaning out of the following car was the swarthy man she had last seen in the toy department earlier that morning, the mysterious Jacques who had frightened the couple who had eluded her.

His dark face looked sinister and for a moment she closed her eyes to shut out the sight.

The taximan repeated his question. "Do you want me to stop? Do you want to join your friend?" he persisted.

"No. Go faster, faster. I will pay you well if you can get away from him," she panted. "Go anywhere, round the back streets. Any place where you can shake him off."

The drive became a nightmare. Looking as though he were enjoying himself, although he was adding to her fears, the man at the wheel sent his car skidding round corners, paying no attention to gendarmes' whistles or even traffic lights when they were against him.

Relentlessly, the other taxi followed, while Sally pressed herself into a corner, hanging on to the window-strap so she would not be hurled from side to side. She had no idea where she was, for this was not the Paris of the shops and big hotels in which she usually found herself.

Eventually the gap between the two taxis widen- ed and, after a few more corners had been taken, the driver grinned at his breathless passenger.

"I think we have won. The other car went straight on at the last traffic lights. You are safe, mademoiselle. What do you want to do now?"

"I will get out," said Sally weakly, realising that she had so little money that she dare not take the taxi any farther. "Thank you for helping me."

She added a good tip to the fare he asked and, shaking a little with nerves, she went into the nearest café to order a black coffee.

The hot drink revived her and she sat quietly wondering what to do next.

Once again Fate decided for her. With a sudden sense of horror, she looked up to find the swarthy Jacques coming into the café and looking straight at her.

She rose to her feet in a frantic effort to avoid him, but the man in the waterproof grasped her wrist and forced her to sink back into the chair.

"You gave me quite a chase," he said, keeping a grip on her. "It was very foolish. You must have known I would find you. Now, where are the other two? And what have you got in that big handbag of yours?"

Sally looked round the café, which was in a poor working-class district and found no face which looked as though it would be friendly. There were only a few rough-looking men at the other tables who did not look at all interested in her plight. One or two, with a quick look at Jacques, paid their bills and disappeared.

She tilted her chin, determined not to be intimidated by the stranger.

"I have my British passport, monsieur," she said proudly. "It will show you that I am a reporter on a national newspaper which takes care of its staff. If you try to harm me it will be worse for you."

To her amazement the man loosened his grip on her wrist and looked at her less menacingly.

"Show me the passport," he demanded.

Hoping she was doing the right thing, she took

the little blue book out of her handbag and, without letting go of it, opened it at the page which showed her name and profession.

"Sally Baxter? I have heard of you," said the man slowly. "Permit me to show you my credentials."

As she stared at the piece of cardboard he offered her, a wonderful sense of relief chased away her fear.

"You are a policeman," she looked blankly. "I thought you were a crook."

"And I was convinced you were one," said the man, smiling for the first time. "Judging by the company you kept today, the mistake was understandable. What were you doing with Marcel Levier, the smuggler, and Madame Mouthier? Tell me all about it over another cup of coffee and a pastry. You look shaken, mademoiselle."

Radiantly happy, Sally told him the whole story from the moment she had found Tom and Mary Inman accused of theft to the frustration she had experienced when the two foreigners had escaped at the airport.

The French detective grasped her hand, but this time it was in a warm and friendly manner.

"Congratulations, Miss Reporter. It is no wonder your name is becoming famous. You have done a wonderful job for me as well as your newspaper. The address you gave me, the Rue Blanc, is the last link in my own investigations. I think that before the day is out your two companions will be locked up. If you will come with me I will take you to the police station, where you can rest and be warm until I have news for you."

It was evening when Sally heard the whole story after the capture of Marcel Levier and the woman in the mink coat.

Madame Mouthier, a Swiss, was new to the smuggling game and had been entrusted with the package of valuable watches to take to London from Paris. She had a rendezvous with Levier in Marshaws' store, where she was to hand over the parcel. Arriving too early, she had been looking round the toy department when she had caught sight of Jacques, who had not spotted her although he had tracked her as far as the store.

Getting into a panic, she had slipped the package into Father Christmas's sack as a way of getting rid of it, feeling she would rather run the risk of incurring the smuggler's wrath than risking arrest by the French detective.

She had returned to Marshaws the next morning, instructed to find out from Santa Claus what had become of the packet, and this time Jacques was close behind her. He had been amazed to find a teenager helping her to escape, but taking the relief plane, he had followed the threesome to Paris, with the result Sally already knew.

"What will happen to Madame Mouthier?" asked Sally anxiously. "I feel rather sorry for her. She seemed to be so frightened."

"Only a light sentence. She is just a silly woman who has got into wrong company, and this is her first offence," Jacques reassured her. "Now, Sally, I know you are anxious to get home. There is a seat for you on the night plane. This time I will drive you to the airport, very slowly and safely."

It was a sleepy but happy Sally who was at Marshaws' store early the next morning demanding to see the manager and placing before him all the typed and signed evidence needed to clear Tom and Mary Inman of the accusations brought against them.

"Can they have their jobs back today and can I be the person to tell them?" she begged.

"Certainly. Assure them we are very pleased and anxious to apologise," she was told.

Later in the day, with her suitcase in her hand, Sally snatched a minute on the way to catch her train to Nashbridge to visit the store which had provided her with such a wonderful story for the *Evening Cry*.

Across the crowded toy department she waved to Father Christmas, whose blue eyes were twinkling as merrily as ever, and caught a glimpse of Mary's radiant face as she bent to catch a whispered address from one of the children who pressed round her table.

She turned away and hurried off to the station. It would be a happy Christmas after all.

PEARL RIVER ADVENTURE

Shirley Flight leaned forward in the taxi, excitement in her blue eyes as she looked out on the teeming streets of Hong Kong.

It was an hour since she had arrived at Kai Tak Airport with a plane full of troops and their families, and now she had three days and nights of liberty — wonderful time in which to explore.

She hugged herself with delight as she looked on the traffic-choked Queen's Road, at the crimson-painted Chinese characters on the fronts of the buildings.

People surged in the middle of the road and ignored the traffic, seeming only to understand the cries of the rickshaw pullers. "'Way 'shaw! 'Way 'shaw!"

At the Oriental Hotel, Shirley paid off the taxi and stood on the pavement, her nose wrinkled as she savoured the mixed aromas of cardamon and curries, fish and incense, which was China.

Case in hand she entered the hotel lobby and stood there for a moment looking around. She was jerked into surprise as a voice at her elbow said quietly: "If I didn't know it was impossible, I'd say that you were Tracy Brandon! Same hair, same eyes, same figure."

Shirley turned to stare at the young Navy pilot a foot or so behind her, cap in hand, his blonde hair and blue eyes oddly at variance with the Orientals around them.

"Lieutenant Geoff Russell, R.N.," he saluted. "I'm sorry to scare you like that, but the resemblance to a friend of mine was so marked that I couldn't help speaking to you."

"I'm Shirley Flight, Transcontinental Airlines," she replied, beginning to move off towards the reception desk.

"Look, we can't talk here," he urged, following her. "And I want to do just that — no," he put out a hand, "I'm not trying to be impertinent, but please will you have dinner with me?"

"I'm afraid that's impossible," Shirley protested. "And I don't think that you have anything to say that could possibly interest me, Lieutenant."

She put down her bag and picked up the pen to register, but was restrained by the desperate look which came into the young officer's eyes, and her curiosity was aroused when he spoke again.

"Please, if you won't have dinner with me, will you spare me five minutes?" he pleaded.

"I shall be dining with my crew," she said, relenting a little. "And before then I have to unpack and shower, but if you'd like to join us at half-past seven you'll be welcome."

A smile lit up his sun-tanned face. "Seven-thirty it shall be," he agreed. "May I bring a friend?"

"I suppose so," she looked at him doubtfully,

anxious to escape and relax in her room for the brief time before the meal.

As she bathed and changed into a cool, silk frock, Shirley wondered about the strange behaviour of the young naval man. "Well, at least," she consoled herself, "I can hardly come to any harm with Captain Evans and the crew around. Perhaps Lieutenant Russell was suffering from too much sun. Perhaps he won't come, anyhow."

Still wondering, she ran a comb through her hair and was ready.

As she entered the foyer she saw that she had been wrong in her estimation of Geoff Russell, for he was standing there by the reception desk, immaculate in his tropical dress uniform, and with him was a tall, dark man of his own age, keen-eyed, but with a worried look creasing his forehead.

The rest of the crew were there, too, and after quick introductions went into dinner.

Clark Brandon, Geoff's friend, sat next to Shirley, but spoke very little, and it was not until coffee arrived that he seemed to relax.

"I'm amazed by your likeness to my sister," he began. "Geoff mentioned her to you, didn't he?"

"Yes." Shirley stirred her coffee thoughtfully.

"I'm a newspaper reporter on the *South China Times* and Tracy's a photographer. We work together, Miss Flight, and I'm so worried about her. She is trapped in mainland China somewhere around Macao, and has a kitful of pictures of men who were prisoners-of-war, reported dead in Korea. Those men are still alive and with those pictures as proof, the government will act to have them restored to their families. Tracy has gone into hiding in the hope that she can smuggle the films back to Hong Kong, but it's three weeks since I heard anything of her, and I'm scared."

As she listened to his story, Shirley thrilled. All about her was the sound of clacking Cantonese accent, and somewhere in the distance a weird-sounding orchestra was wailing out the old tune of "Rose, Rose, I love you".

At last Clark leaned back, it was then that Shirley realised that the rest of the party had been listening to his story.

"Macao! Now, there's an idea," Captain Evans said. "How about a trip to Pearl River? It's Portugese territory."

"Except for the island in the river, sir," Geoff put in.

"There are casinos there just like Monte Carlo," Evans went on. "Palm shaded streets, and it's a nice run on the ferry, exactly like going to the Isle of Man."

"Except for the machine-guns on the ship, and the armed guards," Clark said grimly.

"Don't be a spoil-sport," Shirley reproved. "I think it's a good idea. Could we go tomorrow?"

"We'll all go," Barry Clinton, radio operator on Shirley's flight, smiled. "Macao, here we come."

"Count me out," Clark smiled ruefully. "My

name is mud in Macao. I'll just stay here in Hong Kong and worry myself sick about Tracy. She's a resourceful girl, my sister, but the police in Macao are going to prove much more clever." He lowered his voice as he turned to Shirley. "I'm glad you're going though, you may be able to pick up some news about her."

"Surely the Consulate could get her back without trouble," puzzled Shirley.

"They could, but she'd have to leave the pictures behind and she won't do that unless there's no other way. She wants to help those poor men and she's pretty determined to do it."

"Bring a change of clothing with you," Russell advised as they went towards the lift and their rooms. "It gets terribly hot in Macao, and we'll get hotel rooms so that we can freshen up."

It seemed strange to Shirley to have to take a travelling bag on a day's outing, but she obeyed Russell's instructions and packed undies and a silk dress the next morning. She was wearing her uniform to travel in and when she met Barry in the hall and saw Russell coming in through the swing doors she looked around for Captain Evans.

"The boss can't come," Barry said. "He's been called over to the airport, something wrong with an engine and the maintenance men want him there. He says to be careful and not get into any trouble."

"As though we would," Shirley chuckled.

She thought about the times that warning had

been given to her, and the times she had disobeyed it. Today, she knew, there would be no opportunity to get into trouble, with the tall figures of her escorts acting like guards.

It was a four hour trip from Hong Kong to Macao and every minute of it was packed with interest for Shirley as she watched the sampans going out on their fishing trips, queer, overloaded little craft which looked so frail and yet must have been tough to judge by the amount of tackle and crews they carried.

It was overwhelmingly hot and humid, even on the water where there should have been a breeze, and the girl was glad when at last Macao came into view and the gang-plank was lowered.

This was the East all right, she thought, as she stepped from the upper deck of the vessel and wrinkled her nose at the mixture of smells which arose as she walked onto the dockside. About the quay was a crowd of rickshaw boys waiting for customers. There were hawkers with trays of oriental souvenirs which fascinated Shirley, but she was dragged away by Russell.

"They've probably been made in England," he grinned.

On their way into town, Shirley wondered why they had bothered to come to Macao. After the beauty of Hong Kong it appeared dirty and unattractive and even the couple of modern skyscrapers looming up ahead did nothing to convince her that she was going to enjoy this trip.

She was looking forward to the coolness of the shower and the joy of changing into a thin dress, and when they reached the Grand Hotel was grateful to be ushered to a room on the third floor. The shades were drawn, and the floor cool to her bare feet as she took off her shoes and stockings before she discarded even the forage cap of her blue-grey uniform.

A soft step behind her made her stand a minute, heart thudding before she turned, relief in her face as she saw the small figure of the Chinese girl who stood there, head bowed, hands discreetly hidden in the wide sleeves of the kimono.

"Me maid, Lee Marlin. Come to help Missy unpack. Run bath. You need wash-wash woman?"

Shirley smiled and ran a hand through her damp, fair curls.

"Thank you, Lee Marlin," she said. "But I am only here for a short visit. I do not need clothes washing. You may run a bath for me if . . ."

She drew back as the girl raised her head and stared at her, the dark, oriental eyes wide, something like fear touching the smooth face.

"Missy Brandon," the maid breathed. "How you get away? How you come here? What uniform do you wear? It is not safe, you must go quickly."

Shirley put out a hand in an attempt to soothe the servant.

"Lee Marlin, I am not Miss Brandon," she said quickly. "I am Shirley Flight, an English air hostess here to sightsee for one day."

"I not believe you." Still there was incredulity in the Chinese face. "You Missy Brandon. I know you. You live here for long time. I know you go into hiding after police see you."

"Look." Shirley fished desperately in her zip bag and brought out her passport. "This will show you who I am. Look, picture of me, Shirley Flight. Can you read that?"

It took a full ten minutes to convince the girl that she was mistaken and another ten to assure her that the uniform was not a disguise, and by that time Shirley was becoming more and more interested in the mysterious Tracy Brandon. She was also becoming dimly aware of Geoff Russell's reason for getting to know her. He had booked the rooms at this hotel and must have known that the floor maid would think that her former mistress had come back.

"Lee," she began, when the girl returned from the bathroom where she had been laying out fresh towels. "Where is Tracy Brandon?"

The Chinese girl gave her an inscrutable glance and shrugged. "I not know," she said briefly.

"Yes, I think you do." Shirley faced her. "I would like to help her and I cannot do that if you won't do your share."

"You speak true?"

"Yes, I do."

Funnily enough, Shirley thought as she watched the other girl's face, *I do want to help. My life seems to have become entangled with this stranger's. I know what it's like to be in trouble after all my adventures, and if I can help Tracy then I'm going to.*

Aloud, she said, "Lee, you must tell me where Miss Brandon is so that I can go and talk to her."

The maid studied Shirley carefully for a minute, and then she smiled gravely. "I trust you, Missy Flight. Now Missy Brandon is hiding in far part of town in hotel where my sister works. I told her to go there."

Shirley walked over to the window and looked down on the crowded street. "Will you take me to this place?"

The girl shook her head. "That I dare not do. I tell you name. You go alone. The police they have already spoken to me and they watch me."

"Very well." Shirley bustled around the room, picking up her discarded shoes, hurrying into her stockings with scant regard for ladders. "You give me the address, and . . ." Hurriedly she found her pen and a piece of hotel notepaper. "You see that this note is delivered to Mr Clinton in room twenty-four, if I am not back before dinner to-night. You understand?"

Lee Marlin nodded. "Yes, Missy. I do that." She hesitated a moment, then added, "ask first for Su Marlin, my sister, at the Chu-Ling Hotel, Monthana."

Quickly Shirley wrote the note for Barry, wondering how best to word it, wondering what the men would say when they knew that she had taken off into the teeming streets of this strange town.

"*Barry*," she wrote, "*I have a lead on Tracy Brandon, and I am going to see her. If I'm not back in time to sail, ask the maid on my floor, Lee Marlin. She will tell you where I am.*"

"I think it better for you to stay here, Missy," there was fear in the maid's eyes as she took the envelope from Shirley. "It will need a clever person to help Miss Tracy."

"Don't worry about me." Shirley patted her arm. "I can take care of myself."

But she wondered about that as she hurried out of the hotel hallway, praying that she wouldn't see Barry or Geoff. It was one thing to be able to take care of yourself in reasonable surroundings, but Macao, she knew, wasn't that kind of a place.

She hailed a rickshaw, and as the panting boy pulled it down the main street and quickly away from the brightest lights, Shirley knew a moment of fear.

What was she letting herself in for now? She watched the rickshaw boy forcing his way through the milling crowd of people who disregarded all traffic and wandered aimlessly in the middle of the road.

The streets were growing narrower as they went, and now there were few lights except those in tiny shops, open to the street; where sinister looking Chinese waited by their wares — strange looking foodstuffs, bright cheap clothing and shiny souvenirs all laid out in profusion.

The Chu-Ling Hotel lay in the narrowest street of all, where overhanging buildings, ancient and dirty, almost touched overhead. There was no air and very little light. Shirley shuddered as the boy pulled up before the dingy front of the place.

It was half-an-hour since they had left the Grand Hotel, but to Shirley it felt like a lifetime. She roused herself to pay the boy, and felt as though she were losing a friend as he pattered off down the street.

The hall of the little hotel was brighter than the outside, for it was hung with quaint banners bearing Chinese signs, and the young girl who came forward to greet Shirley was pretty in her flowery native dress.

"I am looking for Su Marlin," Shirley began. "Her sister, Lee, sent me here."

"I am Su." The girl bowed her head, but not before Shirley had seen the quick interest her uniform had brought.

"My sister, I trust she is well?"

"Quite well. Su, I wish to talk to Miss Brandon. Will you take me to her at once? It is urgent. I have little time."

For an instant she thought that Su was going to refuse, but then the solemn brown eyes, meeting hers, reassured her. "You follow me, Missy, please?"

Tracy Brandon's room was at the very top of the hotel, up steep stairs, down uneven corridors then behind two locked doors.

When the second door was opened and Shirley was face to face with the photographer, she gazed at the girl who came forward, amazed.

It was like looking into a mirror, she thought dazedly as she took in the blue eyes, the short, fair hair only a shade darker than her own. Tracy was of the same height, a little fatter, but the resemblance was so marked that Su, who had not shown any wonder in the beginning, now stared from one to the other, her eyes wide.

Quickly Shirley explained who she was, and her reason for being there, and Tracy, recovered from the shock of seeing her double, pushed a chair forward.

"I'll be glad of a new brain," she said grimly. "I just can't think any more. After three weeks of worry I was considering giving myself up to the Consul and letting him get me away."

"What about your pictures?"

"Oh, them," Tracy shrugged. "I tried to do the impossible and hoped it would come off. But the police heard about it and are too interested in me to ever let me get away with the photos I took. I was too nosey, I reckon. Will you go back, Miss Flight, and tell my brother that I'm tired of this and will do anything to be free again?"

"No, I'm not going to do that," Shirley whipped off her cap and handed it to the girl. "There's a better way. Try that on for size."

Dubiously Tracy did as she was bidden, then stared at herself in the cracked mirror.

76

"It'll work," Shirley insisted. "Change clothes with me. Walk out of here as easily as I walked in. Use my passport if you have to and get back to Hong Kong. Take your pictures with you."

"Hey . . . wait a minute." Tracy crossed to where Shirley sat. "You can't mean this. You don't know what you're offering to do. It's wonderful of you, but I can't let you do it. You'll be left here. If the police come they'll question you."

"You've hidden here for three weeks," Shirley argued. "Why should they come now? I'll get away tomorrow, somehow."

"Tomorrow?" Tracy laughed. "Shirley, you're in the Far East now where there can be complications such as you've never dreamt of."

"I don't care," Shirley was stubborn; certain that this was the only way to get Tracy and the films to safety. "Hurry, change clothes with me."

Still the other girl hesitated. "I don't like to get you involved in any trouble," she insisted. "You're very kind and I appreciate it."

"Then get into this." Whilst Tracy had been talking, Shirley had taken off her uniform coat and skirt and was unbuttoning her blouse. "And don't worry about me. I'm perfectly innocent and I'll get away. The important thing is that you must get those pictures back and help those men."

"Missy right," Su put in, holding out Shirley's blouse. "You go."

"When you reach the Grand Hotel," Shirley said as she slipped Tracy's cotton dress over her head, "go straight to room thirty-six. Geoff Russell and my radio operator are in twenty-four. Lee Marlin will contact them. And do hurry because if one of us isn't back by dinner-time they'll all be in a panic. Have you got the films?"

"Yes," Tracy held out a small packet.

"Slip them into the inside lining of the cap," Shirley advised. "My passport is in the pocket of the jacket."

"You know what trouble you'll be in for if this doesn't work, don't you?" Tracy's voice was grim.

"I know. And let me worry about it." Shirley gave her a little push. "Now, go, and good luck."

"You're a wonderful person, Shirley Flight." Tracy, leaning forward, gave the other girl a quick hug and a kiss. "Thank you."

"I'll see you in Hong Kong," Shirley called with a lightness she was far from feeling as she watched the others leave the little room, and heard the key turn in the lock.

Her heart sank as she looked out of the window and saw the Chinese policeman patrolling up and down the narrow street. Had he seen her come into the hotel? Was he waiting to find out what an English air hostess might be doing in this squalid part of town?

She watched breathlessly until the figure of Tracy Brandon, neat and upright in the borrowed uniform, appeared and walked briskly away from the Chu-Ling Hotel to stand on the corner of the street and casually hail a rickshaw.

The policeman stopped and stared for a minute but made no move toward the rickshaw and its occupant. Shirley turned away from the window and sank into a chair, aware that her legs were trembling and her heart thudding with the anxiety of the past few minutes.

There was little to do in the small room except to glance through the books which Tracy had left, and within an hour Shirley was suffering from a bad attack of nerves.

What a fool she had been to hand her passport over to a strange girl. A girl who, through striking resemblance, could take the passport and use it as she wished. Perhaps she would not even go near the Grand Hotel, but take off on some other mad photographic adventure.

Cold shivers ran down Shirley's back and she wanted to scream. Why had she been so impetuous? What on earth was Captain Evans going to say when he heard of this escapade? That he would be angry was putting it mildly.

She began to pace the room, remembering the peculiar circumstances of her meeting with Lieutenant Russell. The whole affair had been a frame-up and she had been silly enough to fall for it.

Doubts and fears chased madly through her brain until, just before dusk, the shy Su Marlin unlocked the door and came softly into the room, carrying a tray.

In spite of her terror, Shirley's mouth watered as

she saw the delicious food which the girl laid out on the table. There were all kinds of tempting Chinese dishes and when at last Su poured out the clear China tea into the handleless cup and handed it to her, Shirley began to feel brighter.

By now, if everything was as Tracy and her brother had said, the other girl must be back at the Grand Hotel and within the next hour on her way back across the ferry to Hong Kong.

She knew that Barry Clinton would hate to go without her and would be working on some kind of scheme to get her back to safety, but she could not think how he would be able to do it without arousing the suspicions of Captain Evans.

It was a struggle to lie down on the hard bed and try to sleep that night, for so many things were harassing Shirley and not the least of them was the fact that by her foolish action it might be a very long time before she saw either England or any of her friends.

"You're a fool," she told herself sternly at last. "You brought it all on yourself, and you know what a good friend Barry is. He'll do something."

She was up early, glad of the chance to stretch her legs and ease her back after the sleepless night on the unrelenting bed. When Su came in with breakfast Shirley saw that the Chinese girl had brought English newspapers. At least they would help to pass the time, but before lunchtime she had read them from cover to cover, including the adverts.

The rest of that day was endless, only broken by the smiling Su when she brought food, and because of her duties in the hotel the girl could not stay to chat.

It was early evening when Shirley, dreading the thought of another night in the confined little room, heard the sound of footsteps and the key once again turning in the lock.

The footsteps were purposeful and ominous and the soft little shuffle of Su's native slippers accompanied them.

It was a scared little Chinese girl who appeared first in the doorway, eyes wide, mouth tremulous. "I bring visitor," she announced fearfully.

Shirley's heart felt as though it were turning over. This was it, then. The police had found Tracy's hiding place at last. She searched her brain feverishly for words to convince the official that she was not Tracy Brandon, and realised at the same time that she had no proof. That all she had to identify herself was the other girl's passport!

Looking up fearfully she met the piercing gaze of — Captain Evans!

Her first feeling was of thankfulness that Tracy had got to safety and that after all her story had been true, but she quailed as she saw the look in the Captain's eyes.

He was carrying a small zipped bag which he handed to her with a curt, "get into these and look slippy," and the look on his face did not soften.

As he turned towards the door he looked back

and shook his head slowly from side to side making a despairing, "Tck! Tck! Tck!"

Shirley straightened her shoulders, trying hard to appear her usual efficient self in spite of the rumpled frock and her tousled fair hair.

"I'll wait outside," he said briefly, and was gone.

Eagerly she explored the contents of her bag. There was her uniform, neatly folded, and in the pocket her passport.

It was a matter of five minutes to change and stuff Tracy's dress into the bag, then to open the door and say in a small voice, "I'm ready, sir."

Evans kept up the silence all the way down the narrow stairs to where Su waited in the hall. "Good luck, Missy," she smiled, showing her even teeth.

"Thank you," Shirley managed to smile back, and then she was following the Captain out into the street.

What had previously been a quiet side street was transformed now, Shirley saw with sinking heart. An army lorry, pulling up at the opposite end, disgorged half-a-dozen soldiers. There was more than one policeman, too, and she swallowed hard as she realised it would only have been a matter of minutes before the men would have been clattering up the stairs of the Chu-Ling Hotel. For it was obvious that the authorities had heard of Tracy Brandon's hideout and were coming to search for her; and for the pictures which they wanted to stop being published.

"Keep your head high and walk quickly," breathed Captain Evans grimly. "If there's any talking to be done leave it to me. I can't think why I should help you but . . ."

He quickened his pace as he spoke, and Shirley found it hard to keep up with him in her high-heeled court shoes. If she hadn't known him so well, she would have sworn that he was enjoying this adventure — maybe, she thought, she didn't know him so well after all.

They passed the army truck and Shirley's heart thudded wildly as the sergeant in charge of the men eyed the English pair curiously. He advanced a step as though to challenge them, but stepped aside when the Captain charged on. Two minutes more, and around the next corner, a car awaited them, and without ceremony Evans thrust Shirley into it. At once the driver let in the clutch and set off at breakneck speed down the narrow streets to pull up with a screech in front of the Grand Hotel.

Still Captain Evans was silent and grim as he hailed another cab and ordered the driver to make for the ferry. "We've ten minutes to catch the night boat," he said, "and if we don't make it, we've had it. Those army men will be on our tails once they've searched that hotel."

All the questions which rose to Shirley's lips were silenced by anxiety as she watched the road behind them, keeping her fingers crossed when the driver was held up, first by traffic and then by the inevitable lazy road crossers.

But at last the quay came into view and she found herself hustled into Customs. Luckily there were few passengers and they reached the deck of the ferry, the last to board as the crew hauled in the gangplank.

She took a deep breath and leaned against the rail watching the dock grow further away as the vessel chugged out into the river.

"There you are," Captain Evans, fanning his face with his uniform cap, pointed to where the army truck crashed to a stop within inches of the edge of the dock, and the men piled out to stand, staring up at the now quickly moving ship. "It was a close thing, and you're the silliest girl I ever knew . . ."

"Please sir," Shirley was determined to ask one question before she settled down to the lecture which she knew was coming and which she deserved. "Is Tracy Brandon all right?"

"Thanks to you, yes. She came back to Hong Kong with Clinton and Russell. Barry wanted to come back for you, but I thought it was my duty to do that. I'm not very good at intrigue, Miss Flight, and the only way I could think of to get you out was the obvious one, in your own clothes."

"Thank you sir," Shirley said gratefully, and was about to apologise further, but was stopped by his hand on her arm.

"You look all in," he said gruffly. "Let's go down for a meal and some coffee. I could use them and I'm sure you could, too. We shall say no more about this little trip, seeing that it's turned out all right after all. But remember, I'm getting too old for rescue work, so next time you're on my flight behave yourself. And that's an order."

"Yes, sir," Shirley smiled up at him, her blue eyes twinkling.

Captain Evans, she thought, was a very understanding man after all.

THE LANDSLIDE

Julie Ross, the youngest travel courier employed by "GO", relaxed in the front seat of the coach as it left Lake Como speeding on towards Locarno in Switzerland. Her passengers were settled after a good breakfast and a wonderful five days in Italy, and Julie eased off her shoes, knowing that from now until they reached their mid-morning stop she could enjoy the scenery.

Now, after one season's work for the firm, the small, dark girl, with the freckled nose and the friendly brown eyes, was more confident, and the party she was in charge of made her more so. For they were all kind people with not a moaner amongst them.

Her driver, Angus Finlay, a young stocky Scot with the reddest hair she had ever seen, was a tower of strength, often going out of his way to help her.

The road ahead unwound upwards like a ribbon, the heat haze already shimmering so that it seemed the coach would soon run into a lake. All around were mountains covered by pine trees and broken only by an occasional house, its windows shining as the morning sun caught them.

Coffee and cream cakes in Bellinzona broke the morning run, and now the route was breathtaking, the mountainous road so narrow that it would be impossible for two coaches to pass. Way down below, many hundreds of feet to the right, was a sheer drop and one or two of the more timid passengers shuddered as they looked down.

Angus, handling the big coach expertly, was singing happily as they rounded yet another hairpin bend, but his song stopped abruptly, and Julie peered up ahead to see what had caused him to slow down.

She gasped as she saw, only a few feet in front of them, the great pile of rocks and boulders which completely blocked the road.

"A wee landslide," Angus whistled through his teeth.

"Now what do we do?" Julie opened the door to climb down on to the road, the passengers following, to stand and stare too.

"We'll have to go back." Angus shrugged. "Take a day to shift that lot. Yes, we'll have to go back and tell the local police."

"But we can't turn," Julie protested.

"Not here," he admitted cheerfully. "We'll have to go backwards until we come to the lay-by."

Julie shivered. "My people aren't going to like that," she said, aware that there was nothing else for it but to try.

Unwilling to accept the driver's decision, she walked over to the boulders and climbed over some of them. It was then that she saw, half buried by the rocks, a car, its bonnet crushed, windscreen shattered. Her eyes grew wide when, moving a little closer, she thought she saw a movement. She looked again, afraid of what she might see.

Something moved again! That made Julie leap into action and she scrambled back to where Angus stood looking down the steep road.

"Angus! There's a car under those rocks and I think there's someone in it," she whispered urgently.

He stared at her. "There can't be anyone alive under that lot."

"Please come and look," she begged.

He followed her down the other side of the landslide where the condition of the car was clearer. There he bent down, pulling at one of the rear doors, struggling to get it open.

They both saw the man who was spread-eagled half-way over the front seat, as though he had seen the beginning of the fall and tried to get away from it.

"I don't think he's badly hurt." Angus wormed his way into the wreck and looked at the unconscious man.

"What can we do?" Julie held the door wide so that the driver could examine the man. "We shouldn't move him, it says in all the first-aid books. . . ."

Angus came up for air and grinned at her. "This is a time we must forget the books, my bonnie," he said briskly. "We've got to get him out of here and bandage that cut on his head. Then we've got to turn the coach around and get him back to a hospital. Don't talk," he added as he saw her mouth open. "Just help me."

Somehow they got the man out. He was small and slim and Angus was strong, so that all Julie had to do was to guide him back to the road. At last they laid the stranger carefully on the narrow grass verge.

"I'll go for my case," Julie suggested. "I've got some first-aid kit. . . ."

The words had scarcely left her mouth when the loud sound of a motor horn made them look up at the next bend in the road.

"Quick!" Angus stood up. "We've got to stop this fellow from coming round that bend and bashing into the rocks."

Julie was the quicker off the mark, and she ran, stumbling in her high-heeled shoes, towards the oncoming vehicle, whipping out her hankie and waving it at the long, continental coach which rushed towards her. Brakes screeched then, and the driver jumped down.

Quickly the girl explained what had happened, noting as she talked that the coach was empty and that it belonged to the same firm as their own.

"I was just on my way with a relief coach," the driver said.

"I know!" Julie had a sudden inspiration. "You could take *our* coach, and my passengers could climb over the rocks into yours. That would save time and neither of us would be off schedule."

"Clever girl," he agreed.

"Not so clever," she smiled. "Just terrified of going backwards down that dreadful road."

It took twenty minutes to turn the coaches and transfer the passengers and their luggage. Then the two drivers carried the unconscious man and settled him on the back seat, with Julie sitting on the floor beside him, praying that they had not made him worse by moving him.

Just as the coach moved off towards Locarno, Julie's eyes were suddenly struck by a bright light which flashed across her face. She stood up quickly, looking back down the road through the rear window, and as she did so she caught the light again.

There was someone up on the side of the hill which fringed the road. Someone with a powerful pair of binoculars! But who? And why? And had they any connection with the landslide?

Who, wondered Julie, was this man who lay so still with the blood already seeping through the bandage on his head? She decided to try to find out, but felt like a spy as she unfastened the brief-case which they had found in the car.

There were some closely typed papers which she did not look at but replaced carefully. Then she found the passport which was different from any she had seen and bore the name of ROBERT ELLIS, DEPARTMENT OF INLAND REVENUE, CUSTOMS AND EXCISE.

The words leapt up at her and Julie Ross knew that she had once again stumbled into a mystery. Someone had wished this man harm and had started the landslide just when his car was passing one spot in the road. There must be a gang, she decided excitedly, for no one person could have caused all that rock to fall.

"One of these days," she admonished herself, "your imagination will land you into real trouble. You're day-dreaming again."

They were within a few minutes of their destination when Robert Ellis moved, and Julie put out a hand to steady him on the narrow seat.

"Where . . . am . . . I?" He opened his eyes and stared at her. "Who . . . are . . . you?"

She smiled at him quietly. "You had an accident. We are taking you to Locarno to a doctor."

He struggled to sit up. "I don't want to go to Locarno," he gasped. "I just left there. I've got to catch three men driving a white Land Rover. . . ."

"I'm sorry." Julie restrained him. "Your head is hurt, and your car smashed by a landslide. Do you remember that?"

He sighed. "I remember. I followed that car. Did you meet it on the road? Did you?"

"No, we met nothing all the way from Como. Look, you must have a doctor and treatment."

"Those men are desperate. I'm a customs investigator, and I've followed them for weeks."

The coach pulled up then at their hotel in Locarno, The Albergo Ticino, and before the passengers were settled, Julie and Angus helped the injured man into a bedroom immediately provided by the manager. A doctor was sent for and, whilst Julie waited for him, Angus coped with luggage and shepherded the passengers into the dining-room.

In no time at all Mr Ellis was expertly bandaged and given pills to ease his pain.

At last he was comfortable, and Julie spoke comfortingly to him. "Mr Ellis, why don't we send for the police and let them find this gang of men?"

"No. It's my job and I'll finish it. The men I followed are part of a syndicate of smugglers taking diamonds from South Africa to Europe. I want their leader."

"Well, another few hours won't matter," Julie soothed, and with that he had to be content.

After a quick lunch she went back and found him sleeping, so she went up to her room and changed into a cool cotton frock and sandals.

Now, she thought, she was prepared for anything. She would have a shot at helping the customs man. Chasing dangerous smugglers was hardly her idea of fun, but she felt so sorry for Mr Ellis, and she had two free days.

Walking out into the busy street, Julie wondered about her next move. How on earth was she to find the whereabouts of a white Land Rover? Then she remembered that there would be dozens of coach-drivers here with their parties and she knew from experience that they congregated at a little café tucked away in a side street.

As she made her way to the Apollo she was glad

to be free and out of uniform. It was hot and sunny and she felt almost like a holidaymaker as she strolled along, stopping once to admire exquisite Swiss pottery figures in the windows of a very modern shop.

She found five drivers whom she knew, but all of them shook their heads when she asked them about the car. Disappointed, she sat down at the only available table over by the service door, and ordered tea and cakes. She may as well wait and see if anyone else came in. "Don't be impatient," she told herself, "you may not even be lucky enough to find one clue. Two days isn't very long, and Mr Ellis told you he was dealing with clever and ruthless smugglers."

Idly glancing around, she saw the tall, elegantly dressed woman come in and be conducted with ceremony to a table obviously reserved for her. Julie stared enviously at the expensive, immaculate white dress, the dark hair styled in the newest fashion, but most of all she was attracted by the woman's steel-grey eyes which seemed to see everything at once, penetrating and commanding.

Julie beckoned to the waitress. "May I have some more hot water, please?" Then she added idly, "Does that woman in white live here? She is very beautiful."

The girl smiled. "She owns the pottery shop and has a studio where she designs. Her name is Selma Kroll."

Julie remembered the shop where she had

stopped, and then her attention was taken by the appearance of a slim young man dressed in local costume. He carried a guitar and, circling the tables, began to sing. Julie watched him absently, and then keenly as he drew level with Miss Kroll's table. Was it her imagination or did a sharp glance pass from those grey eyes to the brown ones? Hadn't his hand stopped strumming long enough to meet briefly the scarlet-tipped one of the woman?

Then, as he finally slipped out of the service door after his act, and stood there acknowledging the applause, Julie's heart began to thud wildly.

For she could clearly see through the wide window beyond the door, the white Land Rover parked at the back of the café!

She called for her bill and thought about her next move impatiently as the waitress seemed deliberately slow. She must get back to the hotel and tell Mr Ellis what she had seen. Then he would certainly have to let the police handle the case, for he wasn't fit to do it.

Julie ran back down the streets, bumping into people, almost being knocked down by cars. At the hotel, without waiting to knock, she rushed into Mr Ellis's room, and then stood, eyes wide with astonishment, as she saw the empty bed, clothes flung back as though the man had left in a hurry.

"Oh, heavens," she said aloud. "Perhaps he's worse and they've taken him to hospital."

Fuming at the waste of time, she made her way

to the office, but the manager was as suprised as she was.

"He hasn't left here, I'm certain," he assured her, going to the empty room to stare about him perplexed. "I came up to see him an hour ago. We shall have to call the police. . . ."

"No, please," Julie put a hand on his arm. "Not just yet. I think I may be able to find him. Don't ask any questions but give me a few hours."

"Well," he looked doubtful. "It's most irregular, but . . . I'll do as you ask. I hope you know what you're doing."

So do I, thought Julie ruefully. Oh, so do I.

She wandered disconsolately out on to the veranda, her mind a muddle of plans which she discarded as soon as she thought of them.

When she saw Angus walking towards her she could have hugged him. Here was someone she could talk to. Perhaps he would be able to help.

He listened to her story with the hint of a grin on his sunburned face, but he had grown serious by the time she was finished.

"Let's go back to the café," he suggested. "That's the best thing to do. We can plan as we go."

Waiting to cross the busy road, Julie's attention was taken by the shabby old man who stood by the doorway of a shop directly opposite to the hotel. He looked so inconspicuous, but somehow had an air of mystery about him. He *seemed* disinterested in the passers-by, but yet he glanced up quickly each time anyone left the building.

"Come on, lassie, stop your day-dreaming or we'll never get across," Angus's broad accent brought her back to her senses, and she allowed him to lead her into the maze of traffic and to safety on the other side of the road.

"Let's take a wee walk around the block," he suggested when at last they reached the Apollo. "Then we can see if the car's still there."

She agreed eagerly, but they were both abashed when they saw the high wall which surrounded the rear of the place.

"There's a gate," Julie said tentatively. "If we could open it just a crack. . . ."

"Someone'll see us and think we're going to rob the café." Angus sounded dour.

"Oh, all right, if you're scared. . . ." Julie marched up to the gate and tried the heavy latch. It gave way and she found herself peering intently through the three-inch opening.

Angus stood behind her, breathing heavily down her neck, and in spite of herself she gave a low chuckle. "Stop breathing," she whispered. "It tickles!"

They both saw the Land Rover then, and in a startled instant heard its engine roar into life. Julie felt as if she were rooted to the spot. For the man in the driving-seat was the guitar singer!

Just in time, Angus wrenched the gate shut and tugged at her arm. They ran back down the alleyway to stand panting outside the café.

"We've got to follow him," the girl said urgently.

"On our own four feet?" Angus was scornful. "Wait. I know a chap at the garage around the corner. I'll nip there and borrow a car. It'll take a minute or two for that fellow to open the gate. You watch his direction."

"Do hurry." Julie watched him go.

It was ten minutes before the Land Rover came out, turning on to the road which led out of Locarno, and Julie wondered what had happened to Angus.

Fifteen minutes, twenty. It was too late now. Furious at the delay, Julie walked towards the street where Angus had gone. There was no sign of him.

She stared back at the café and there, sitting at a window table, was the old man who had been standing across from the hotel. Who was he, and what did he want? She wondered about him vaguely, worried about the disappearance of Angus.

It was late afternoon when she finally admitted to herself that the coach-driver was not coming back and she made her way back to the hotel, hopefully.

She was relieved to find that the manager was off duty so at least she wouldn't have to answer any awkward questions about Mr Ellis, who still had not returned to his room.

Julie changed for dinner feeling as though the sight of food would choke her. But she managed to eat a little and was cheered by the appearance of

one of her fellow "GO" couriers who breezed into the dining-room for a quick meal before taking her party on to a show.

"Saw old Angus half an hour ago," the girl said.

"Where did you see him?" Julie demanded.

"In a smashing car with a beautiful brunette. They were driving up the road towards Appensea — you know, the deserted village. Hey, where are you going?"

Julie sat down as quickly as she had stood up. "Nowhere," she said dully. But what, she wondered, had made Angus desert her and go off with Selma Kroll, for it was obvious that she was his companion.

Neither of the men had returned when Julie went reluctantly to bed. There seemed to be nothing else to do. At midnight she was still awake, and in desperation she got up and dressed. Slipping a light woolly over her thin dress she went outside. Again the old man was over by the shop and the girl had a wild idea that he might be watching her. Hurrying down the road towards the lake, she stood at last looking out over the water, the reflection of the mountains and the twinkling lights.

It was then that she heard a car stop on the narrow roadway and the soft voice of a woman. "Miss Ross, I believe?"

Julie turned and saw Selma Kroll. In the back seat was the man who had played the guitar at the café.

"Your friend Angus has had an accident. He would like to see you."

"See me?" Julie was poised for flight, but she was too late. Strong hands were on her arms and before she could utter a sound she was pushed into the car.

"Let me go! Let me go!"

The couple took no notice and Miss Kroll drove the car swiftly up the narrow road and into the village, which Julie recognised as Appensea, for she had brought many of her tourists up here.

The car stopped before an old, deserted house and Julie was bundled out, up steep stairs and pushed into a moonlit room.

"Angus!" She ran to the figure over by the window.

Quickly he told her how he had been taken away in the car by a man who flourished a revolver. How Miss Kroll had brought him here.

"Listen," he ended. "There's a plane coming tonight to pick this gang up. Miss Kroll is the boss. The guitar singer and the pilot of the plane have been doing the smuggling for her. We got too interested, that's why they captured us."

"We've got to get away," Julie determined. "But how? Oh, Angus, that's a plane circling now."

Suddenly she clutched his arm. "Below this window there's a parapet and below that a flat roof. Could we . . .?"

He grinned. "I reckon we could. What's a broken neck between friends? But it'll mean breaking the window and that's going to make a terrific noise."

Julie whipped off her cardigan and smiled. "Take off a shoe to break the glass, and blanket the sound with my woolly," she said urgently. "We can't waste any time."

Her heart felt as though it would burst as she waited for Angus to do the work which could mean freedom. It would be awful if their captors came along now and stopped them.

But at least the sound was dulled by the thickness of the cardigan and in a matter of minutes they were out on the narrow ledge. It was a good thing that it was dark, Julie thought as she tried to avoid looking down. At least it hid the dreadful drop to the hard ground.

Cautiously she followed the driver along the ledge. There was no sound from their captors and the girl kept her fingers crossed as she edged forward.

"I'm going to jump now," whispered Angus. "When I say go, you follow me."

Dazedly she obeyed. How on earth were they going to stop the criminals now that they were free? They had no way of getting into town, and she realised for the first time what a hopeless task they had set themselves.

It seemed an age before they were on the ground, standing for a moment to peer helplessly about them. Then Julie snapped her fingers excitedly.

"Angus, I've got it," she said. "I know how we can delay that plane. Then you can go for help whilst I wait here. Come on."

"Just a minute," he panted after her.

"I haven't got one to spare." Julie rushed on, taking advantage of the cover of the trees towards the field where they could see the outline of the plane.

"We're going to let the air out of those tyres," she flung the words back over her shoulder.

They were stumbling on over rough stones and somehow over the wall into the field. Then the aircraft loomed above them and they began their task. A loud hiss came from Angus's side as the tyre deflated and Julie struggled on to release the valve on her side.

But even as she accomplished the job they both heard footsteps on the cobbled road.

"They're coming. We've got to hide." Angus was anxious.

"You go." Julie gave him a push. "Bring anyone you can find." She ran for the shelter of the trees.

The two men and Miss Kroll came into view almost at once, each carrying a small case, and the girl watched as they climbed into the plane. She heard the engine turn into life and saw the dim outline of the propellers as they began to turn.

With bated breath she waited for the pilot to find why the craft wouldn't taxi, but it was five minutes before the engine stopped again and the passengers climbed out to inspect the machine.

They walked round with flashlights and she heard their exclamations as they located the trouble.

"We should have *punctured* the tyres," she realised suddenly. "Then they couldn't have mended them quickly. As it is they can pump them up or something."

Julie was so deep in thought that the brilliant light of a flashlight glancing about the field, catching her hideout, blinded her and made her aware that she had been discovered. Too late she tried to run farther, out of that searching beam of light.

It was then that everything seemed to happen at once.

The field, a second ago so silent, seemed to be full of uniformed men, dark forms all advancing on the aeroplane and the three people who stood transfixed by it. Julie heard Angus's voice calling to her and she moved towards the sound, thankful that he had found help in time.

But the first person she recognised as she ran towards the leading party was the old man who had been so mysteriously following her.

Now she knew him and ran to him, laughing and crying with relief. He was Mr Ellis!

It was almost daylight when the three of them finally sat down to a late meal in the deserted dining-room of their hotel.

Julie, so tired that she could hardly keep her eyes open was excited by the capture of the smugglers, and Mr Ellis, now changed into his own

clothing, a small plaster over the cut on his head, was triumphant.

"My department will never be able to thank you enough for what you have done today, Miss Ross," he smiled.

Julie blushed. "If you hadn't come along with the police . . ." she began.

"It was a good thing you weren't depending on me," said Angus. "Meeting Mr Ellis and the others was a stroke of luck. I couldn't see anyone around *to* help."

"One thing I would like to know, if it isn't a great secret," Julie went on, "is how it all started."

The customs man stirred his coffee thoughtfully. "It began many months ago," he began. "We knew that diamonds were being smuggled out of South Africa and into Switzerland and Italy but we couldn't find the method until one day in the customs shed. . . ."

Julie leaned forward, fully awake now. "Go on," she prompted.

"One of our men, examining a passenger's luggage took from it a porcelain figure and dropped it. It was Swiss and was of William Tell shooting the apple from his son's head. That apple contained a diamond. Well, we arrested the man who was carrying it, but he wouldn't give away any of his associates."

Julie gasped and Angus whistled softly.

"The figures, we have now found, were made by Miss Kroll and smuggled out by her agents. She made one big mistake and that was to keep the models all alike. We confiscated several, but not all of them held diamonds. She never sold this model in her shop so we could not pin our suspicions on to her. But now, thanks to you, we know."

He pushed his empty cup towards Julie and, like someone in a dream, she picked up the coffee-pot and replenished the cup.

"I had to get out of the hotel and adopt my disguise because I knew the gang must know of your inquisitiveness, and I had to let them go to the limit in order to catch them. But even I was worried when I saw them take you off in that car. I was scared that something dreadful would happen to you."

"It almost did on that parapet," Julie chuckled. "I hate heights."

"You're a brave girl." Mr Ellis patted her arm. "But even heroines must sleep and you're off to bed this instant or we'll have to carry you there."

"I won't sleep." She stood up stiffly. "But I've got a conducted tour to do tomorrow, so I suppose I'd better make an effort."

"You had that." Angus took her arm gently. "And mind you keep out of trouble for a while now."

"I'll try my best," Julie promised, but she knew that when the next adventure came along she would be ready!

MYSTERY ON CANVAS

Mallery Cane and Lucille Fair lugged their suitcases and painting kit down off the rack, and waited until the train stopped in Chilbury Station. Then they climbed down on to the platform of the little country station and breathed in the fragrant country air.

Mallery sniffed delightedly. "Oh, how wonderful it is," she cried. "It looks like spring here, and it smells like spring."

She then turned to lead the way out of the station and into the little forecourt, where a collection of farm transport was parked. An antique country bus stood in one corner, and an even more antique taxi-cab stood at the pavement edge waiting to pick up fares.

The two girls hailed the taxi and loaded their belongings into the back, while a couple of leisurely porters heaved their trunks on to the luggage rack at the back and roped them on.

After a casual and cheerful chat about the weather and the prospects of a wonderful summer, the girls climbed aboard, and a minute later the taxi was roaring up the narrow high street of Chilbury and up the winding hill to Chilbury Castle.

The castle had recently been converted into a school of art, and was already proving to be a great success.

When Mallery and Lucille had reached school-leaving age, they had persuaded their parents to allow them to enrol at the Chilbury Castle Art School for two or three years and to receive expert coaching from the proprietor, Monsieur Carrilon, the famous artist and critic who was running the establishment.

The taxi eventually reached the top of the hill and crawled round the massive walls of the castle, and over the drawbridge, and so into the grounds.

Monsieur Carrilon was waiting in the ancient stone carved doorway beneath a coloured stone crest and he smiled a cheerful welcome, while the hall porter and the taxi-driver took the girls' belongings up the wonderful oak staircase to the room that the girls were to share during their life at the school.

Mallery and Lucille were escorted to their room by the proprietor, and they cried out in delight when they entered the delightful room that had been allotted to them. The walls were oak-panelled, the floor was as smooth and mellow as honey, and the curtains and chair-covers were gay with brightly flowered chintz. The linen fold oak furniture perfected the tastefully decorated room.

"Lunch will be served in just fifteen minutes," Monsieur Carrilon informed them. "It will be in the Tudor dining-room. There you will meet your fellow-students."

After a delicious lunch of cold roast ham and fresh salad, followed by caramel custards and fruit tarts and fragrant coffee, Monsieur Carrilon rose to his feet and made a little speech of welcome. He ended by saying: "On this first afternoon of the new term, we shall all spend the time together in the famous art gallery, and I shall explain special points about some of the paintings to you and answer any questions that you may care to ask. Afterwards you will be invited to wander about at will to study and examine the paintings, or make sketches of anything that takes your fancy. Your studies will be based on your own 'bents' and individual tastes."

The art gallery proved to be sheer delight, for the glorious old paintings seemed to glow in the sunshine that poured in through the windows that lined the long outer walls, and the highly polished oak floor and panelled walls shone like glass, whilst the great refectory table in the centre of the room was filled with antique silver that bore the seasoned bloom of well-loved and well-cared-for treasures.

Monsieur Carrilon showed his thirty-five pupils round the gallery, and then left them to do their sketching and painting.

Lucille planted her easel and stool and paints at a good vantage-point; it was by a window at the end of the gallery that overlooked the valley and the lake below, and for a while she was too absorbed to see what Mallery was doing.

Lucille worked away for twenty minutes and then she noticed with surprise that Mallery was still

moving about the gallery, her tackle still not set up and lying stacked neatly in one corner.

But Mallery was not wandering idly about. She was seriously and systematically searching for something, and Lucille began to watch her with growing curiosity. She was longing to ask Mallery what the mystery was, but she knew better than to ask. Mallery could close up like a clam if questioned about her own private and personal affairs.

Suddenly Mallery began to examine an old sword that was lying on the refectory table in its scabbard. She slid the blade out of its sheath and examined it carefully, and then, putting it down quickly on the table, pulled a sketching block and pencil out of her pocket and made a very painstaking sketch of the blade.

Lucille turned her attention to her painting, but half an hour later she observed that Mallery was busy making a sketch of a large painting of an interior of a room in some old house.

Lucille worked on for a while, and then she wandered over to her friend and picked up her sketch-book. "How are you getting on, Mallery?" she inquired. "What's this design in your sketch-book? What is the motive behind it, or is it supposed to be something in the abstract?"

Mallery had risen to her feet when Lucille had approached, and seemed rather furtive about something. She pulled the sketch-book out of Lucille's hands and said: "I'd rather you didn't see that, please. It's . . . well, it's a secret. Please don't ask any questions."

Lucille bit back an angry retort, but thought better of it and remained silent for a few moments. When she did speak again, she spoke of the work that Mallery was doing and carefully kept the conversation off her own efforts.

As the two girls chatted, Mallery carefully put her sketches away in her folder and tied it up securely. She then began to work on an entirely different subject, and Lucille teased her about her secrecy.

"Don't tell anybody about those sketches," pleaded Mallery. "I don't want them discussed or criticised."

When the session had concluded, the students went to the lounge next to the gallery, where afternoon tea was served. As the two friends rested and took their refreshments, a dark-haired girl walked over and introduced herself.

"I'm Norma Billet," she said, her voice dull and toneless.

The two pals introduced themselves and invited Norma to join them for tea, although they were not very impressed with her. Her smooth black hair was beautifully glossy, but her looks were spoiled by her long, thin face, tight-lipped mouth, and narrow eyes. Her lack of expression, both vocally and facially, did nothing to add to her charms.

Norma looked keenly at Mallery and said: "I

saw you sketching something from the armoury department. Are you particularly interested in swords and bayonets?"

Mallery flushed, but quickly hid her feelings. "I was just fooling around," she replied with mock cheerfulness. "I like to sketch a few oddments just by way of 'warming up' before I start serious work."

Norma watched her over the rim of her tea-cup.

"You took quite a long time to 'warm up' today, didn't you?" she said curiously, her keen eyes searching the other girl's face. "May I see the drawings?"

Before either of the girls could stop her, she grabbed Mallery's folder, untied it and spilled the sketches out on to her lap. Mallery rose to her feet in anger and snatched the drawing of the inscription from Norma's hand before the girl had time to really see what was down on paper. Mallery gathered up the remaining sketches and the folder, put the papers away and re-tied the folder securely.

"I'll gladly show you any sketches that you may wish to see if you but ask," she said coldly, "but I prefer to show them to you myself. I don't like people to help themselves."

Norma jumped to her feet in a temper. "Sorry you've been troubled," she cried, and she flounced away from them in a rage.

At dinner that evening the two pals found themselves sitting almost opposite to Norma Billet, but

the dark girl was decidedly cool and only nodded a brief greeting to them. Over coffee, Norma began to hold a very serious conversation with her next-door neighbour, a young man who had been introduced to the pals earlier on as Clavering Pastell.

Clavering was curiously like Norma in appearance. They might almost have been brother and sister. They glanced at the pals from time to time as though they were talking about them. The glances during the close conversation rather gave the show away.

Mallery retired rather early that evening, saying that she had one or two letters to write, but when Lucille followed her up to her room an hour later, she was amazed to find that Mallery was not in the room.

Lucille looked in the wardrobe to see if her dress was hanging there, but was even more surprised to find that Mallery's outdoor clothes were not there either.

She had no idea where Mallery had gone, and so all she could do was to wait anxiously for her to return.

Lucille's anxiety grew as she heard the loud thud of the massive oak front doors being closed, a squeaking and scraping of the old lock as the key was turned. The shooting of bolts set her pacing up and down in a frenzy of worry.

Where had her friend gone to so late at night, and why had she gone out without telling even her best friend?

It was not until twelve o'clock had struck on the town hall clock that Lucille saw a dark figure hurrying in through the gateway that was, fortunately, left open all night. The figure paused under a lamp, and Lucille breathed a sigh of relief as she recognised Mallery.

Mallery looked up at their bedroom window, and Lucille signalled to her with a flashlight. Five minutes later, Mallery had climbed up the ivy-covered drainpipe and in at the first-floor window.

"Wherever have you been, Mallery?" cried Lucille, angry now that her anxiety had been dissolved. "Why don't you tell me what's going on? What are you up to? I've never known you to be so secretive ever before in all the time I've known you."

Mallery sat on the edge of her bed until she got her breath back, and then she said: "The whole thing is so secret, and so important, that I cannot tell anybody the full details, not even you."

Lucille waited in angry silence for her friend to continue.

"I am looking for something," went on Mallery after a slight pause, "that will make a broken life into a new and bright one. I had a hunch about something, but now I know that it is more than a hunch."

Lucille suddenly felt ashamed of herself for her outburst of temper, and said gently to her friend as she looked down at her: "It won't hurt anybody if you tell me the outline of the story. I would be able to help you and I will definitely not divulge any part of your secret to anybody at all. You know that you can trust me."

Mallery remained silent for a few moments, and then she said: "There is a special sword in this castle, and I have just had it proved to me that I have found it. There is a special inscription on the blade, and it contains a clue. The remainder of the clue is mixed up with the interior I was sketching this afternoon. The person most concerned in this matter is staying in Chilbury and I have been to see this person. We have worked out the clues, and now all that remains to be done is to find that room. My friend has found an old book about the castle, and that room is right here under this roof. Somewhere. We must find that room and solve the mystery."

"I'll help you all I can," said Lucille, patting her chum's shoulder. "Don't worry, it will all come out right, whatever it is."

"Today," said Mallery thoughtfully, "I have also discovered that two other people would like to solve that mystery too. They would bring ruin to my friend if they could, and take everything for themselves. Those people are Norma and Clavering. I can't tell you any more yet, Lucille, but we must find that room before they do."

Suddenly the bedroom door was opened and Norma Billet walked into the room, a deep scowl on her face. "What are you doing with a light on at this time of night?" she snapped. "Don't you know

that it is well after midnight? Why aren't you un-
dressed and in bed asleep?"

"I might ask you the same question," replied
Lucille curtly. "We had a few letters to write, then
we read a little, and we were just having a talk
before retiring for the night. We are not at school
now or under school rules; this school of art is
quite a different thing. Our free time is our own,
and you have nothing to do with it."

Norma was plainly taken aback by the stand put up by the girls, and she was at a loss to know how to deal with the situation now.

"I will say nothing this time," she muttered, "but if I catch you two up to any more peculiar moves, I'll report you."

"That goes for you too," snapped Lucille. "Now please leave our room. When we want you in here, we will invite you."

When Norma had left the room, Mallery said: "Now we've got to get moving, and quickly too. I'm sure Norma was listening outside the door."

"We have to find that room tonight," said Lucille, "but how are we going to start? We can't go round the castle from room to room seeking it. That would be impossible."

Mallery gave a little secret smile and produced a shabby book from her pocket. It was the *History of Chilbury Castle*, and contained maps and drawings. Mallery opened it at a page and showed Lucille a drawing. The page showed a drawing of a room. It was identical with the room in the painting. The caption read: THE SMALL DINING-ROOM.

"I caught a glimpse of it this evening," whispered Mallery. "The door was open as I was going out, ostensibly to post a letter. The room is used by Monsieur Carrilon as his private study. We will go and investigate."

Silently the two girls crept down the stairs and into the oak-panelled room, with its wonderful carvings. Mallery produced the two sketches and showed Lucille a special piece of carving on the drawing. The item took the form of a tiny shield bearing the inscription that was also carved on the sword blade.

Mallery and Lucille stared round the room at the various shields that were carved out of the woodwork between each panel, and then began to systematically examine each shield.

"The inscription is on one of these shields," said Mallery, "and somewhere behind the panel, probably in a small secret recess that is opened by a spring, is the other half of the clue."

The minutes ticked by as the girls explored the carvings, working silently and intently. The opening of the door startled them to such an extent that Mallery slipped and fell back against the wall.

Norma Billet and Clavering Pastell burst into the room, followed more sedately by Monsieur Carrilon himself.

"There are the thieves," shouted Norma, pointing excitedly at the two pals. "I told you they were up to no good."

"Not so fast," cried Monsieur Carrilon. "I happen to know a little more about this matter than any of you think. I believe that the young lady here has found the answer to quite a problem."

He stepped up to Mallery, and pointed to the panel behind her. Her fall had accidentally touched a knob, a spring had been set into operation, and the panel had slid back, revealing an elaborate piece of carving hidden away behind it for several generations.

A large yellow package lay in a niche, and Monsieur Carrilon picked it up with a cry of joy. "If my information is correct," he informed them, "here are the deeds of the castle. They will prove definitely and conclusively who the castle really belongs to. Looking at the crest there, I see now that it does not belong to Norma Billet's family. It belongs to the Cane family. Mallery's family. But we shall soon see."

Monsieur Carrilon opened the dusty package and revealed a pile of ancient documents, and he proceeded to go through the papers carefully. The watchers scarcely breathed as he read through the papers.

"It is as I thought," he said, at last. "The Canes are the rightful owners of the castle. It fell into the wrong hands by a trick. You see, besides being an artist, I am also an historian, and when I leased this castle, I read up everything that I could find about it. I read that the castle had fallen into the wrong hands by a trick, and the Billets were not the rightful owners. Norma found out that Mallery was one of the Chilbury Canes. I found that out myself when she enrolled herself as a student here, and Norma has tried to prevent Mallery from finding these papers and the remainder of the proof. Legal proof will be needed, but I do not need that to establish her identity. Just look at this painting."

A small canvas was unrolled and revealed a

painting of a lady standing before the newly revealed carving on the wall. The clothes were Elizabethan, and the lady's face was the image of Mallery's face.

Mallery and Lucille were so engrossed with the painting that they almost missed Norma's next move. The girl snatched at the deeds and rushed to the fire that was still burning in the grate. But Monsieur Carrilon dived towards her and seized the documents and the painting.

"Oh, no you don't," he shouted. "I think you and your half-brother would be well advised to pack your bags and leave these premises immediately. If you ever show yourselves round here again, I shall inform the police."

The following morning, Mallery's father brought his solicitor to the castle and definite identity was proved.

A few weeks later, the new owners of the castle gave a garden party in the grounds for all the students and their parents and friends, and Monsieur Carrilon was the guest of honour, being the tenant of the castle.

Lucille squeezed her friend's hand.

"I see now why you were so keen to enrol here instead of a London art school," she said.

Mallery smiled and replied: "The original clues have been in our family for ages, but we didn't know it. If dad hadn't found that old book in a second-hand shop, we should never have got to the bottom of it."

A CASE OF SWAP

Despite the over-hot compartment, Janine Lewick shivered and wished the long journey were over.

Who else, she taunted herself, staring out into the black, rain-blustery night, would be so absurdly nervous at having to spend Christmas with strangers?

What if the Berrijohns had only invited her so that her mother could accompany Professor Berrijohn on his African lecture tour. Wasn't it a tribute to her mother that of all the people on the books of the secretarial agency Professor Berrijohn had considered *her* most competent to replace his sick secretary?

She ought, Janine told herself severely, to be feeling glad at her mother's success, not screwed up with apprehension and home-sickness.

So her clothes *were* home-made, and her last winter's boots scraped. And the Berrijohns *did* live in a big Georgian house in the country, and had a son at university and a daughter at boarding school. That wasn't likely to make them less welcoming or likeable, was it?

She wished the compartment had not emptied at the last stop. Fellow-passengers would have diverted her attention from her stupid self.

How endlessly black the night seemed! Incredible to discover, with a glance at her watch, that it was barely half-past seven. If the train were running to time, she would be at her destination in ten minutes. She rummaged in her handbag for her ticket.

Abruptly she was not alone. A suede-gloved hand appeared round the door and, smart zipped case first and shabby grey case last, a tall girl in a black trouser suit struggled in from the corridor. Quietly the girl slid the door to, and, having flung her zipped case up into the rack, she dropped into the seat opposite Janine.

"Filthy night," she observed. "You going to Osborough?"

Janine shook her head.

"Pity. I was hoping for company."

Not wanting to appear unfriendly, Janine briefly explained.

"I'm a long way from my folks, too." For a moment the girl did *not* look self-sufficient. "Got a mom and kid brother back in Wisconsin. I flew into Birmingham airport this morning."

Janine's surprise showed. Why fly to Birmingham if going to Osborough?

"Had to make a call en route," the girl explained. "Little place called Deriden — an inn there."

She stiffened suddenly as a male figure passed along the corridor. Then, visibly, she subsided with relief.

"Had a queer character in my compartment back there. That's why I made a change. Thought for a moment. . . .

"Just hope I make my Osborough hotel all in one piece, that's all," she added cryptically.

Janine had no time to comment, for they were sliding past blurred platform lights. She began fumbling with the door.

"I'll hand out your case," offered the girl.

Into the light spilled by the carriage windows walked two young figures: one bearded, the other trailing wind-tangled blonde hair.

"Janine?" A welcoming hand shot out. "I'm Roger Berrijohn. This is Fran."

Janine, struggling to release her umbrella, which had somehow become jammed in the door, managed to remember Fran was his sister.

Wind, nerves and a particularly steep step mischievously combined to make her descent from the train a disastrous one. The wind clouted her emerging head, gleefully possessed itself of her woolly hat, and whirled it and a newspaper sheet before it.

Janine, making a futile grab at her hat, lost her balance, and sprawled in mortification at the young people's feet.

A concerned Roger had her on her own feet and dusted down in an instant, while his sister collected the spilled contents of her handbag.

"There, that seems to be everything!" exclaimed Fran.

A shout came from the ticket collector who had obligingly stamped the hat back to earth.

"Come on." Fran took her arm. "Roger will bring your case. Sure you're not hurt?"

Janine shook her head. She had, she felt, made quite enough of a fool of herself without confessing to a twisted ankle.

They emerged into the wild wetness of a country road.

"We're parked under that lamp," said Fran. "Let's share the back seat, shall we?"

Janine felt grateful for the Berrijohns' modest car. Roger, who had stayed chatting with the ticket collector, shot her suitcase into the boot and slid into the driving seat.

"I came to meet you," Fran explained, "because Roger has to drop me off at the church for a carol-singing session, and it seemed mean for no one else to be at home to say hello."

"Well, Mum will be home — just," said Roger, sending up a sheet of water as they rounded a corner. "She has a charity whist drive over at Chabley."

Janine wondered uncomfortably from what activity her arrival might be keeping Roger.

Another sheet of water hit the window; the lamps became fewer, the road rougher.

Roger stopped the car with a jerk.

"Have a cosy evening with Figgy and Mr Talisman," said Fran, as she left them to battle her way up the puddled path to the church.

Janine wondered who Figgy and Mr Talisman were. But she had no chance to ask, for Roger was busy greeting other arriving carol-singers.

"Me?" He grinned at her question as he set the engine going again. "No, I've nothing special to do except pot the Christmas tree, hang the holly and streamers, and blow up about fifty balloons. You can help me, if you like."

That made Janine feel better.

Moments later they had pulled up before the lighted porch of what appeared to be a not too terrifyingly large house. Roger leaned across and thrust open her door for her and, wincing, Janine forced herself to stand on a foot that painfully objected to even her slight weight. Roger vanished towards the boot.

From inside the house came a frenzied barking. The front door flew open, and Janine was suddenly being commanded to come in and mind Figgy.

"My dear, what a horrid night, and how nice to see you."

That was all that Mrs Berrijohn, trailing a stole, managed to say before Figgy himself exploded into the hall, all wildly wagging tail and leaping paws.

Janine staggered back at the delirious welcome. Though young, Figgy was weighty. Instantly she tried to cover up her involuntary cry of pain by stooping to rub the black tummy, for Figgy always concluded his welcomes by slithering on to his back, paws limply upheld in blissful anticipation.

Mrs Berrijohn, however, having a rugger-playing son, had a practised eye for the injuries the young tried to conceal.

Having heard Roger slam the boot, Figgy had bounded noisily into the night to impede *his* progress.

Mrs Berrijohn piloted her now hobbling guest into the lounge, and pushed her into the depths of a cosy chair by the fire. Blushing, Janine had to confess her accident.

"Take Janine's case up to her room, dear," ordered Mrs Berrijohn, en route across the hall to the kitchen for water and lint. "Get down, Figgy!"

Figgy, who at this stage would have eaten lint as joyfully as he ate biscuits, did not get down, and so was hooked by his lead on the door handle. Instantly he slumped to the carpet in soulful submission.

"Helps him get control of himself," said Mrs Berrijohn. "Hm, that ankle is nicely swollen, isn't it? It must be better in time for my Boxing Day dance, dear."

Janine said determinedly that it would be fine by tomorrow.

Roger came in and unhooked Figgy, who promptly chased a spitting Siamese cat on to the back of a sofa. Barking, he then began a dance of advance and retreat that the Siamese, feeling safe, pretended not to notice.

"Mr Talisman," introduced Roger.

Mr Talisman leapt delicately on to a crowded Jacobean sideboard.

Janine realised that Mrs Berrijohn was offering to get her slippers from her case for her. She began a fruitless search in her handbag for the key.

"I must have lost it on the platform!" she exclaimed, in dismay.

Roger grinned. "Not to worry; I'm a practised picker of locks."

"Your supper," said Mrs Berrijohn, having found her son a necessary piece of wire. "Have it by the fire, with the dog shut in the kitchen. Otherwise he'll eat spoons, serviettes and all. Devoured two boxes of figs the first night we had him. Fortunately without disastrous results . . ."

She noticed her son dithering in the doorway. "Well, Roger. . . ?"

"Er, Janine, your slippers. . . ."

Janine saw that he had not found them. "Sorry," she apologised, "I should have said: Mummy rolled them in my dressing-gown."

He still looked uncertain. "You did only have *one* case?"

"Yes."

"A grey one?"

"No," said Janine, in surprise. "Blue."

"Wait a minute." He vanished stairwards.

Mrs Berrijohn straightened the Christmas cards Mr Talisman had knocked over, and bore the cat towards the kitchen for his supper, with a jealous Figgy in her wake.

Roger plonked a shabby grey case on the sofa and silently held back the lid.

At the contents Janine's astonishment grew. A greasy pair of old trousers, an R.A.F. cap, a pair of old seaboots, what looked like a ragged piece of sail, a pipe. . . .

"I—I don't understand." Horribly it was dawning on her that she had no dresses, nightwear, not even a flannel.

"But *she* gave it to me," said Roger.

"She?" exclaimed Mrs Berrijohn, who had joined in the contemplation of the contents.

"The girl sharing Janine's compartment."

Janine's bewilderment increased further. Yes, of course, she recognised the case now. It was the one the trouser-suited American girl had kept on the seat beside her. But why would she have travelled all the way from Wisconsin with this rubbish?

"Sure she was American?" queried Roger.

"Well, she said she was."

"Confidence trick," pronounced Mrs Berrijohn. "Janine's tumble from the train gave the girl just the opportunity to swop a suitcase of junk for Janine's case."

"But she didn't seem that type," protested Janine. "Oh, I only spoke to her for a few moments, yet. . . ." She was remembering the girl's flight to her carriage; her start of fear when someone had walked down the corridor. "Maybe in the confusion she just got muddled."

"My dear, they never do seem the type, or they wouldn't get away with their mean tricks, would they?" said Mrs Berrijohn. "No address or anything inside, I suppose, Roger?"

"Not a thing." Roger turned over a moth-eaten jersey.

"What about *your* case, Janine? Was that labelled?"

"Mummy tied one label on the handle, and stuck another inside the lid."

Mrs Berrijohn glanced consideringly at the grandfather clock. "The train must have arrived in Osborough twenty minutes ago. If it was a genuine mistake, the girl might have left Janine's case in the Lost Property."

"Let's find out," said Roger, promptly going to the telephone in the hall.

Janine listened anxiously, but the clerk at the other end of the wire was obviously being adamant. No blue suitcase, bearing a label printed Janine Lewick, had been handed in that evening. Only an umbrella and two odd gloves had come in off the Midlands train. No, considering how near Christmas it was, he was *not* particularly busy; certainly not too busy to forget anything that had happened during the past half hour.

"I wonder," said Janine as, against a background of despairing canine howls, Mrs Berrijohn brought in Janine's supper-tray, "if the girl might contact me here direct? I think, if I were her, I'd prefer to put the matter right that way."

"Well, she might," conceded Mrs Berrijohn. "Anyway, my dear, you are not to worry. You're not so much smaller than Fran that you cannot borrow some of her things, and there will be shops open in Candlewell tomorrow. We'll see you are not a Cinderella for Chistmas.

"Now I must fly. Worth waiting for as I am, the whist drive must start before midnight. Roger, there is no need for you to struggle into your raincoat. I can drive myself."

"For the car's sake, *no*, Mother," said Roger firmly. "Hello, where's my scarf?"

"I suspect the dog's had it," said his mother. "You shouldn't take after me and leave your things lying about."

The scarf, somewhat wet and minus several tassels, was retrieved from under the sofa.

"Figgy's favourite sanctum," explained Mrs Berrijohn. "It'll be a relief when he's too large to get under there. Enjoy your supper, Janine, and go to bed early. And, Roger, if you do decide to tackle the Christmas decorations, keep Figgy away from them. I don't want him full of tinsel and balloons."

"As if it would make any difference to *that* stomach," grimaced Roger.

Figgy's frenzy, roused by the sounds of their departure, subsided, and Janine sipped coffee and explored under the serviette-shrouded plates. Despite her lost suitcase and throbbing ankle, she was very hungry.

She would finish her supper; carry the tray back to the kitchen; and release Figgy. . . .

Shrilly, insistently, the telephone in the hall demanded to be answered. For greater speed, Janine hopped her way to it.

"Is that you?" came an agitated female voice. "I mean, are you Janine Lewick, the girl I met on the train?"

Janine felt both relief and pleasure. The girl *had* contacted her.

"Yes, you gave me the wrong case . . ." she began eagerly.

"You've still got it?"

"Of course."

"Thank goodness." There was a heave of relief. Then: "No listen, I — I didn't give you the wrong suitcase. I mean, it wasn't a mistake. I swopped the cases deliberately."

Uneasiness and a draught sweeping suddenly under the front door sent a little shiver down Janine's back.

"I don't understand. . . ."

"I had to do it, honey. Can't explain fully because I don't know the whole of it myself yet. Remember I said there was a queer guy in my compartment? Well, that wasn't so either. But I *was* being followed. And when the women sharing my compartment went along to the refreshment car, I knew I had to find another compartment quick. Or risk *him* moving in. So I shot in with you.

"Now, the point is, honey, it could be dangerous for you. He's got your address. I tore up the one tied on your handle, but soon as he saw your case he realised what I'd done, and then of course he found the label inside your lid. I'm sorry about that. If I'd known. . . ."

"He?" Janine's world was rocking.

"This smoothie in the trilby hat who tried to pick me up in the *Green Man* at Deriden, then followed me on to the train. I've no idea who he is, but he wants that case; it's obvious. And he mustn't get it, honey. I've travelled a heck of a long way to collect that case, and. . . ."

"Do you know what it contains?" cut in Janine curiously. If the girl did not, she was in for a big disappointment.

"Nope! And it's not mine to open. Oh, it's a queer story. . . .

"You're not alone there, are you?" she exclaimed, in sudden alarm.

Frighteningly Janine realised she was.

"Well, be careful," warned the girl. "Keep the doors and windows locked. I'll explain all I know as soon as I can get to you."

"Are you coming tonight?"

"If I can get a taxi to bring me that far. Gee, the crack that guy gave me on my cranium didn't help. I don't think the walls of this room ought to be going round the way they are."

"Look, why don't you ring the police and let

them handle it?" said Janine.

"Police!" Janine could not tell if the girl sounded surprised or startled. "N — no, I'd better not. At least not until I know. . . .

"You just keep that case *and* yourself safe, honey."

The girl rang off, leaving Janine uncomfortably aware that an innocent person, acting normally, would have contacted the police instantly. Especially if they had been hit over the head.

With a further tremor of trepidation, she realised she did not even know the girl's name.

Oh well, she had better find a temporary hiding place for the case. But first she was going to look through its ill-smelling contents again. There might be something interesting Roger had not noticed.

Janine hobbled into the lounge. Figgy's release, which he was loudly demanding, would have to be delayed a few minutes longer.

Carefully she shook out each article, felt and peered into the boots, discovered — in the pocket of the trousers — a damp-soiled snapshot of what looked like two pilots in flying kit. Nothing of value in there, though — that was for certain.

She closed down the lid, and snapped the catches shut.

The front door chimes pealed sweetly. Janine's blood promptly congealed. She thrust the case under the sofa, and, as the bells chimed again, hurried as quickly as she could to get Figgy. His boisterous barking might just be wrongly interpreted.

Holding his lead firmly — for he was as anxious to have the front door open as she was reluctant — Janine turned back the catch.

However, it was no sinister man in a trilby dripping rainwater on to the porch tiles, but a little woman shrouded in plastic from her hood to her overshoes.

"I've called to collect the Roof Fund Envelope," she beamed. "Mrs Berrijohn did promise. . . ."

Janine, struggling to retain control of Figgy, found the sealed envelope on the hall table. The woman stuffed it into a leather bag.

"Such a beastly night! But work must go on. . . ."

Shooting up her umbrella before her as a shield, she paddled back into the elements. Headlights lit the gravel-drive, and the little woman had to draw in suddenly against the darkly massed bushes.

Janine's gasp of relief died; her throat tightened; for the car drawing up before her was not Roger's.

Her cry to the woman was drowned by Figgy's fresh storm of barking.

The driver's door opened, and Figgy determinedly tore his lead free of Janine's grasp. Of this caller he was not to be deprived!

Emerging hands firmly resisted the dog's welcome, and caught up the trailing lead.

"Miss Lewick?" The man's voice was polite and reassuring, like his tweed overcoat and pipe. He was *not* wearing a trilby.

"Police." He held out a card which Figgy promptly leapt to devour. Laughing, the man hurriedly pocketed it. "Don't think my chief inspector would approve of you having that, young fellow. May I come inside a moment, miss? It's about that rather odd encounter you had on the train this evening."

Janine, her eyes on the familiar blue suitcase he had taken from inside his car, nodded. If he was from the police, it must be all right, mustn't it?

The man secured Figgy's lead to the hall door knob. "There, chappy. Business first, eh?"

A thwarted Figgy was left lying on his back.

The man turned to Janine. "There was a practised smuggler travelling on that train. Er, would you prefer someone else to hear this too?"

Janine, fear beginning to hammer again, had to confess she was alone. But someone would be returning any minute, she said defensively.

He nodded, as if it were of no consequence.

"One of the Revenue men was tailing her. Unfortunately she realised this. Gave him the slip. She shot into your compartment, I understand, and exchanged her suitcase for yours. Highly delighted with herself over that little trick. What she hadn't realised was that your address would be inside the lid. . . ."

It all seemed to fit. Maybe the girl's apprehension had been due to a Revenue man on her tail. Maybe she had not been hit over the head at all.

"D — did the man arrest her?" Janine knew if the man replied yes, he would be lying.

But he shook his head. "No grey suitcase, no proof, miss. We'll get her one day, but not this time."

Janine remembered the odd contents of the grey suitcase. "W — what was she smuggling?"

"No idea this run, miss. She's clever, that one. She's no doubt got something financially reward-ing in the lining of the false bottom."

Lining — false bottom. Janine had not thought of that.

"Anyway, miss, here is your case. Like to check that all is correct?"

Janine, her hands shaking a little, checked. All was neatly correct.

"Then if I might have the other case, miss, I'll be off."

As Janine hesitated, his voice hardened: "The case, miss."

Involuntarily her eyes had slewed round to the sofa. The man laughed. "Keeping it safely tucked away, were you, miss?"

Outside a horn bleeped a friendly warning of arrival. Tyres scraped on the gravel. Roger!

Violently the man kicked the grey case from its hiding-place.

His haste, combined with his rough — "Get

back!" — to Janine, roused all her only half-squashed suspicions. He was not from the police!

As he pounced upon the case, she grabbed the handle and, though in the ensuing struggle he dragged her halfway across the room, she held on grimly. The tug-of-war ended abruptly, and for Janine, disastrously. Suddenly she was toppling backwards, clutching on the handle. In annoyance she flung it from her.

Meanwhile the man, triumphantly clasping the case, rushed into the hall. A howl from Figgy told of the dog being violently booted from the door. There followed the crash of the front door itself.

Collecting herself into one piece again, Janine hopped into the hall. Figgy was now transporting himself frantically, and Janine had quite a battle to get the door open.

She looked out upon a rapidly vanishing tail-light. Then she saw Roger doubled up over his own bonnet.

"Who the devil . . .?" he gasped, when he could speak at all.

"He said he was a policeman. He's stolen the case."

Roger tore open his driving-seat door.

"Wait for me," said Janine.

An indignant Figgy, wildly twirling about on his lead, had succeeded in shutting the front door for them.

They roared out of the drive and into the blackness of the road.

"Sure to have headed for the main road, I should think," said Roger.

But there was no certainty of it, and when they reached the main road, which way?

"If he hadn't seemed so normal and polite at the beginning I wouldn't have been taken in even a little bit," moaned Janine.

"Did he really have a police card?"

"I — I don't suppose so. I didn't see it properly. Figgy. . . ."

Much later, Figgy received them back joyfully, but Roger and Janine were too concerned with the night's events to pay much attention to a young Labrador going wild with an old slipper or something.

"We'd better ring the police," said Roger.

"But the girl doesn't want them to know. She. . . ."

"Back on the girl's side, are you?" grinned Roger, ruefully massaging his sore ribs. "Point is, Janine, part of what that man said could be true. Maybe the girl is a smuggler. Maybe she did have something valuable stowed away in the lining of that case, and he, being in the same business, knew of it."

It was certainly possible, and it would explain why she did not want the police involved.

"Deriden!" said Janine suddenly. The girl had said the man tried to pick her up in the *Green Man* at Deriden.

"Then let's check if she was there," said Roger. "That can't hurt."

He began dialling directory enquiries.

"The *Green Man* . . ." came a pleasant male voice.

Roger handed over the receiver to Janine. "Manage?"

She nodded.

The new landlord — he had only taken over the inn a couple of weeks ago, he explained — could not have been more helpful.

Yes, he remembered the American girl. She had called to collect a case. Ordered some coffee, then bounced off to catch a train. A queer business altogether. Did she know about it?

Janine said she did not.

Well, the case had been left at the *Green Man* a year ago by an eccentric convalescent. Little man with a ginger beard.

"You know the type: distrusts lawyers, doctors, bankers, politicians . . ."

According to Mrs Coote — she was the previous landlady — the eccentric had been a pilot during the war; twice decorated for bravery. A real mad hat! Hadn't been able to settle down afterwards. Lots of men hadn't. First he'd knocked about with a flying pal of his. They had even had a go at sailing round the world, but their yacht had capsized in a freak storm. After that, it seemed, the friend had married, but the eccentric had drifted into one half-baked adventure after another. A bout in a gold mine had ruined his health, he declared.

Wealthy, Mrs Coote thought he was. Didn't have to stint himself.

Suddenly, his convalescence not finished, he had announced he was off to search for his pal. He had no idea where he was living except it might be in America. Yes, he had agreed with Mrs Coote, he could advertise, but what adventure would there be in that for him? What if he did cut short his life? Wasn't he dying of boredom anyway?

So off into the blue he had gone. All Mrs Coote had had from him was one postcard.

Janine directed the landlord back to the suitcase.

Ah yes, the eccentric had asked Mrs Coote to keep the suitcase at the *Green Man* in a safe, dry place. One day, he told her, someone would arrive to claim it. If that person possessed a key that fitted the lock, the case was to be handed over without questions.

"And today the girl arrived with the key?" said Janine.

"That's right."

"Ask him if she seemed at all nervous when she left," whispered Roger.

"Quite the reverse," said the landlord decidedly.

"Seems her story *is* true, then," said Janine, replacing the receiver. "She probably wouldn't have realised until she got to the station — or maybe until she was on the train — that she was being followed."

"I suppose her father is, or was, the old flying pal the eccentric set out to find," mused Roger. "Yet why would he have left him a case full of old junk? Sentiment? Revenge?"

"I think something valuable *must* be hidden inside it." Janine swallowed apprehensively. "That girl is going to be furious. She will have flown across the Atlantic for nothing."

Roger was about to retort that Janine hadn't asked to have the case dumped on her when there was the sound of a car in the drive. He went quickly to the curtained window.

Car doors banged.

"A man, and a girl in a trouser suit," he reported.

"Oh golly!" Janine's hand flew to her mouth.

Figgy, who had been having one of his quiet spells in his sanctum, hurled himself noisily into the hall after Roger. Janine remained tight in her chair, trying to summon courage for confession.

The slam of the kitchen door told of Figgy being temporarily disposed of.

"Now maybe I can hear what you were saying . . ." Roger ushered in the two visitors.

"Hi!" The girl raised a hand in greeting to Janine. "Oh, I'm sorry, this gentleman your dog tried to eat, he's Inspector Sawson."

Janine and Roger looked doubtfully at each other.

"He's genuine," the girl assured them. "I found him at the Osborough Police Headquarters."

There was a moment's embarrassment, which the inspector himself broke by suggesting that the girl — Miranda Pearson — told them all she knew of tonight's business.

"Well, there's not much *I* know really." She sank into one of the low chairs near the fire. "Like I told the Inspector, a few weeks ago a funny little guy with a ginger beard turned up on our doorstep in Wisconsin and asked for my dad. Said he and my dad had been pals till. . . ."

She glanced half-amusedly, half-warily at the Inspector.

"Oh, what the heck! He's dead," she said. "You can't imprison him now."

The Inspector looked startled.

"Well, years before he apparently got mixed up in some diamond smuggling. That was why he and my dad quarrelled. Dad was all for adventure, but not for breaking the law. Anyway, Mom had to tell him that Dad had been killed in a street accident. The little guy just collapsed at hearing that. The doctors said Mom was not to blame; he had a bad heart condition anyway."

Miranda swung a blue-shod foot. "He never became fully conscious again. But after his death they found a letter. It said there was a suitcase to be collected at the *Green Man*, Deriden, England. The contents — all of them underlined — were for Dad and his family. There was money for the flight and a key. Nothing else. Oh, except he'd written that Dad would know where to look for the really important item. . . ."

"But this man who followed you," said Janine. "Did he know about all this?"

"Not about my end of it, he didn't," said the girl decidedly. "I didn't like the way he tried smarming over me in the *Green Man*. Thought I'd given him the slip; but I hadn't, had I?"

"And you've no idea who he was?" asked the Inspector, who was making notes.

"Nope, 'cept that he said he'd known the little guy who had left the case. I reckon he must have, too, otherwise how'd he have known the case even existed?"

"He could have eavesdropped. Perhaps on you and the landlord, or when Mrs Coote told the landlord about it."

"Maybe. I guess he hoped the case contained something real valuable."

"Smuggled diamonds, for instance?" suggested the Inspector.

Miranda flushed with dismay. "Gee, I hope not, else my Mom won't touch it. Anyway," she

beamed upon them all, "let's open the darned thing and find out, shall we?"

Seeing the quick interchange of glances between Roger and Janine, Miranda exclaimed: "Hey, that guy hasn't been here already, has he?"

There was nothing for it but to tell all. The girl flicked away all Janine's self-blame.

"Oh well, what me and my family didn't get, I guess we won't miss.

"Whatever it was," she added wryly, "it was all my own fault for getting you involved in the first place."

She managed a grin.

"Let's have the hound of yours in, huh? Guess he'll disperse the prevailing gloom."

In came Figgy, delighted to see them all again; out of the Inspector's hand went his pen. Immediately the Inspector stooped to retrieve it, but Figgy was well practised in the art of snapping up desirable playthings. With just a little difficulty, he wriggled to safety under the sofa.

Roger went down determinedly after him, and, despite snapping jaws that never closed hurtfully anyway, managed to get hold of something. Not the pen, though . . .

"Ugh, what on earth is that?" he exclaimed, flinging out something slimy with much chewing.

"Miranda's case handle."

Miranda herself picked it up. "I don't know

153

whether to keep it as a memento or fling it on the fire," she said.

"What's that poking out?" said Janine. "Lining?"

The Inspector held out an imperative hand for it. "Not lining," he declared. "This handle. . . ." Hastily he broke the remaining stitches. "There!" He drew out a thin roll of paper. "Concealed, unless I'm much mistaken, in the cavity where once smuggled diamonds reposed."

Miranda's eyes shot wide. "Jeepers!" Shakily she managed to smooth the paper out. "This being the last will and testament," she read huskily . . . "Twenty thousand . . . to Samuel Pearson or family. All this, I swear, honestly earned . . . Oh, my gosh!"

Roger, with the Inspector's pen, Figgy, with a disintegrating tassel, emerged from the sofa together. It was Figgy, of course, who knocked over the soda water that Janine was hurriedly pouring for a white-faced Miranda.

"Janine, bless you for holding on to the right end of that case," said Miranda, "and Figgy, bless you for chewing it."

When Mrs Berrijohn returned, she noted the glasses and mince-pie crumbs.

"You've had people in. How nice! That must have cheered a dull evening for you both."

Roger said nonchalantly: "Oh, Mum, we've another guest coming for Christmas."

"Good! Do I know her?"

"Her name is Miranda; she's American."

Mrs Berrijohn, however, was no longer listening. With a fast hardening eye, she was surveying a suspiciously fat — spasmodically hiccoughing — Figgy.

"Roger, how many decorations has that dog eaten?"

"None. I'm afraid he just got to the mince-pies first, that's all. But Miranda said he'd earned them."

"Then Miranda can take him for an extra walk tomorrow. I won't have a dog of mine that shape!

"Now, Janine, about a nightdress for you."

"I have my own," said Janine happily, and, to the accompaniment of whistling purrs from Mr Talisman, who had condescended to occupy her lap, she related the whole story.

MYSTERY IN THE WELSH HILLS

The tall, fair-haired girl stood clutching her hold-all and stared at the country folk around her. Some stood, talking in an unknown tongue; others hurried by with secret, withdrawn faces. Cars passed. Some riders on mountain ponies rode carefully. But the expected bus made no appearance.

Jenny Deverell studied the creased sheet of paper, which she clutched like a talisman. Aunt Megan had written the time of arrival of the over-night coach from the Midlands at the bus stop beneath the castle walls.

"This must be the place," thought Jenny. "The bus can't have gone. I was here twenty minutes early. There isn't even a queue. But I daren't ask, it's like being in a foreign country. Aunt Megan didn't say everybody would be talking Welsh."

Suddenly she felt she was being watched and, looking up, she met a pair of laughing, brown eyes.

"Waiting for the bus, are you, then?" asked the tall, dark boy standing beside her.

"I am. I was. Has it gone?" asked Jenny, worriedly.

"No. It's a bit late like because it's Friday," came the astonishing reply.

"Friday," puzzled Jenny.

"You're a townee as well as being English," grinned her companion. "Friday's market day here. The farm women come in with their produce for market. Folk don't hurry in the country."

"Oh!" Jenny digested this information. Then she said, "The bus is late, but there's no queue."

This brought another burst of merriment. "'Course there's no queue. Nobody leaves town on market day except people like you and me, going to spend a holiday on a farm. You are, aren't you? Which one?"

"I'm going to stay there." Jenny brought out her instructions again, and pointed. She dare not try to pronounce the Welsh name, for she was sure that there'd be another guffaw.

"*Mynydd Byhan*," he read. "Not hard to say, really, and I wouldn't have laughed."

Jenny blushed. Heavens, this boy was a thought-reader.

He continued, "That's Auntie Beti. I'm staying next door, over the trout stream. There's a bridge."

Confused, Jenny had a wild vision of two houses joined by a bridge with a stream between the walls of the houses.

"So you're Mrs. Jones' nephew," she said.

"*Chwarchog mawr*! Sorry, that's just an expression like 'Good Heavens'! Auntie Beti's everybody's auntie in Trefon village. Somebody motherly and popular is always called Auntie in Wales. Come on, here's the bus."

The bus creaked up, and out of it came a frenzy of farm wives. Some wore their Sunday best; others wore dark skirts and home-knitted cardigans — but all carried baskets of home produce for the market.

"In with you," said the Welsh boy. "Give me your bag. Mind if I sit with you?"

"I wish you would. I'll be lost if you don't. I'm Jenny Deverell."

Sitting beside her, the boy said, "I'm Alun Williams. I know it's all a bit foreign to you. I went to Liverpool once; it was terrible. Relax! We both get off at the bridge. Then across a field, and you'll be at Auntie Beti's"

"Does Auntie Beti speak English?" asked Jenny nervously.

"Bless you, yes. Not like a television announcer, of course."

As Alun and the conductor spoke soberly in Welsh, Jenny thought about the bridge. It was evidently an important landmark. The conductor passed on.

Alun stared ahead, worriedly and silently.

There was something wrong, thought Jenny. At last she asked, "What's wrong? Shouldn't I be on this bus, or something?"

"Sorry." Alun pulled himself together. "The conductor told me that my grandfather — I'm going to stay with him — has lost over a hundred sheep. They've just disappeared."

"Sheep wander, don't they?" volunteered Jenny. "Couldn't that be it?"

"It must be," Alun smiled weakly. "It's a hill farm, with acres of hilly slopes with sheep all over the place. I'll hear the details when I reach *Felin Ddu* — that means Black Mill," he said, with a ghost of his old jauntiness.

The narrow, twisting road wound its way into the mountains.

"Look!" exclaimed Alun. "There's the bridge." He pointed at a small, humpty bridge.

Jenny stared. "That?" she murmured.

"Did you expect a span like the Severn Bridge or the Forth Bridge?" asked Alun teasingly. "Grandfather says the Romans built the first one here. He's probably right."

The bus slowed down, and then stopped. Joining Alun on the humpty bridge, Jenny looked around.

"Is that Auntie Beti's?" she asked, pointing to a pink-washed farmhouse that clung to the skirts of a small hill.

"That's *Mynydd Bychan*. It means Little Hill. Welsh names always have a meaning," explained Alun. "I'm the other side of the bridge. *Felin Ddu*'s in a hollow by the old mill pond. I'll call and see you and Auntie Beti later."

"Thanks, I'd like that, and I hope those sheep

turn up," said Jenny, smiling. She felt she'd made a friend in a strange land.

Running down the small field was a dumpling of a little woman, followed by two sheep dogs.

"Welcome, Jenny," she called.

Seeing Beti Jones, Jenny understood the Auntie Beti bit — the little woman simply bubbled over with goodwill. The dogs cavorted round Jenny, but at a command from their mistress they headed for home.

"Late again, that old bus," panted Auntie Beti. "Twice I've been to the bridge. I just went back to put another kettle on the fire. Hungry you must be, coming all that way. And how is Megan Price then? Megan Deverell now, of course."

"Very well, thank you," replied Jenny. "She sent her love, and said . . ."

"To make you light-cakes, with my rhubarb jam, for tea," giggled Auntie Beti.

"How did you know?" asked Jenny, laughing.

"I know Megan," came the reply. "Who was that standing with you on the bridge then?"

"Alun Williams," replied Jenny. "We met by the bus stop."

"A clever boy, Alun. Passed top to the Grammar School, did Alun. Mad on climbing and potholing. Not natural, going underground like that is."

The farmhouse overlooked a small orchard of old apple trees. The house had one long front room which was the kitchen. Here an old oak dresser displayed shining lustre china; a black oak settle faced the huge fireplace, where glowing log embers kept the huge black kettle boiling.

Panting, Auntie Beti lead Jenny up the steep stairs to her bedroom. "I'll go down and put a meal on the table now," she said. "Bacon and two eggs, is it?"

Jenny was enjoying her bacon and eggs when the biggest man she'd ever seen entered.

"My husband, Ifan," introduced· her aunt. "Any sign of *Felin Ddu*'s sheep?"

Sadly, Ifan shook his head. "We've covered the mountain, and searched the old quarry."

"They've wandered," said Auntie Beti firmly. "You know how stupid old sheep are. One jumps, and they all jump."

"The bus conductor told Alun," said Jenny. "I thought they must have wandered."

'"Nobody knows how long they've been lost," worried Ifan. "But for the shearing round-up nobody'd have counted them, scattered as they are on the hills."

That afternoon, as Jenny watched Auntie Beti bake her famous light-cakes on her girdlestone, the dogs outside set up a joyful barking.

"Come in, whoever you are," called the little woman.

Seeing Jenny's surprise at this unconventional

invitation she smiled. "It's a friend. Watch and Smart don't bark like that for strangers."

In walked Alun.

"Hello, Auntie Beti," he said breezily.

"Smelt the light-cakes, I suppose," came the swift reply. "Only my fun, boy. Your grandfather heard anything about those sheep?"

"Nothing good," replied Alun. "Evans the Police called."

"The police," exclaimed Jenny, wide-eyed.

"It's daft, like something out of a western," continued Alun. "But Evans thinks it's rustlers."

"Light-cakes won't wait for the police or rustlers," said Auntie Beti placidly. "Sit down. Butter and jam on the table."

Obediently Jenny and Alun buttered and jammed their batter-cakes.

"Rustlers, indeed," said the little woman scornfully. "That's daft talk. Too much television Evans the Police has seen."

"Cattle have been taken in lorries from the lowlands near the main roads," explained Alun. "So . . ."

"So! No lorry could go up those mountains," interrupted Auntie Beti.

"Couldn't they have got the sheep to the road below?" asked Jenny.

"Sheep bleat and fuss, and sounds carry far up here. It's so quiet." Alun addressed himself to Jenny. "The highest point a lorry or a horse-box

could go is a rough road with cottages along it, and they've heard nothing."

"Helicopter," suggested Jenny.

"I thought of that," replied Alun. "But it couldn't be done."

The dogs barked a welcome again.

"Ifan," said his wife, and fairly leapt to her girdlestone.

"Heard you were here, Alun," Ifan remarked, as he scraped his boots on the mud-wiper by the door. "Beti, Evans the Police was asking if we'd seen a funny little townee round here. Anybody called here in the last month selling something?"

Deftly turning her light-cakes, Auntie Beti replied, "Only old Biddy, the Irish gipsy, and Mick the tramp. And Biddy didn't have sheep in her basket, or Mick in his sack, I don't suppose."

"Why? What did this chap look like?" asked Alun hurriedly as he saw Ifan flush at Beti's sarcasm.

"Short. Bowlegged like a jockey. He always wears a checked cap because he's bald except for a ginger fringe round the side and back."

"A lot of old nonsense," scoffed Auntie Beti, plonking a plate of light-cakes on the table. "That old television again — turned Evans the Police's head, for sure. Such a man couldn't be."

Jenny cocked an expressive eyebrow at Alun.

"Why this little man?" asked Alun, turning to Ifan.

"According to 'information received but not proven', as Evans puts it, such a little man was suspected of the cattle thieving in the lowlands."

"That's enough silly talk," warned Auntie Beti. "Talk sense about something else."

Alun cleared his throat. "I wondered if Jenny would like a climb up the mountains tomorrow."

Jenny's eyes sparkled, and she nodded.

"No going down those old potholes, remember," warned Auntie Beti. "It's responsible for Jenny's safety I am."

"No potholes, I promise," grinned Alun.

It was sunny, with a fresh breeze, when Jenny and Alun set out the following morning with Alun carrying a packed lunch.

"Good climbing weather," remarked Alun, as they took a stiff mountain sheep path. "Not too hot."

Looking up at the steep gradient of the mountain track ahead, Jenny asked, "Why this route?"

"There's a splendid view from the top," said Alun.

The view was certainly worth the climb. Sheep dotted the slopes and, below, the isolated farmhouses looked like dolls' houses. An occasional goat stared indignantly at the intruders.

"What's that big house down there?" asked Jenny, pointing.

"An old manor house. Not grand enough to be a

stately home. But the gardens are special. They're open to the public — complete with peacocks. Let's go down and play tourists. I'll treat you. You deserve it after that climb."

"I pay for myself," said Jenny firmly. "Dutch treat or nothing."

Alun grinned. "And you English say we Welsh are proud!" he remarked.

Jenny was surprised to find several other visitors roaming the extensive gardens.

"Where are the peacocks?" she asked Alun.

"By the marble folly and the statues. This way. Drat! Ben the Post has seen me. I must stop and talk. Go straight on. I'll follow as soon as I can."

Jenny followed the path Alun had pointed out through clumps of trees. Then, suddenly, the silence was shattered by the raucous cry of a peacock, and there, on a well-kept lawn surrounded by marble classical statues and a mock castle, paraded the peacocks.

Jenny stopped to admire them. Then she saw she was not the only one interested in the peacocks.

Creeping stealthily towards them was a little man. It was he who had caused the peacock to cry his angry screech. Even though the little man was bent double there was no disregarding his bandy legs, or the checked cap perched on top of a fringe of ginger hair. Jenny stared. It *must* be, it *was* the little man that the police believed to be a rustler.

"*Coo-ee! Coo-ee*, Jenny," carolled Alun, crashing through the trees.

For all the world like an elephant, thought Jenny. She laid a finger on her lips, and ran to meet him.

"The little ginger man Ifan spoke about — he's chasing the peacocks," she whispered.

Together they raced to the peacock lawn — but there was no little man, only a family of outraged peacocks.

"You came crashing like an elephant, and yodelling," snapped Jenny.

"I'm sorry." Alun was truly penitent. "But it could be anybody with red hair. Red hair is very ordinary round here — descendants, they say, of the red-haired bandits that used to terrorise this countryside."

"With bandy legs and a checked cap?" asked Jenny, crossly. "I tell you he was the wanted man. He's finished with cattle rustling. He's moved up into the peacock class."

Tactfully, Alun stopped arguing.

"I'll tell Evans the Police," he promised.

Even Auntie Beti and her husband were not impressed by Jenny's tale of the bandy red-haired man and the peacocks.

"See what you've done — made Jenny believe in rustlers and red-haired scamps." And the little woman rubbed away vigorously at some invisible dust.

Alone with Jenny, Ifan said, "Beti is scared. She always gets hoity-toity when she's frightened."

Next day, Alun called again.

"I saw Evans the Police," he told Jenny. "That little man was over the border in Shropshire yesterday."

"Did they get him?" asked Jenny.

Alun shook his head.

"So," replied Jenny, "maybe the Shropshire folk were mistaken, jumping to the conclusion that any redhead could be the rustler. It might still have been him I saw, though I'm only an English townee," she added.

Alun stared. Then, laughing, he said, "Nothing wrong with being an English townee. I'm a Welsh country bumpkin and I'm not complaining."

"Sorry, Alun. I'm silly. But . . ."

"You saw the wanted man. I believe you. Maybe we'll both see him and catch him next time. Let's go through the forest and come out on the mountain."

The silence of the forest restored Jenny's good humour. They left the spruce and the firs and stood on the hilly slopes, listening to the bleating of sheep.

"Your grandfather's?" asked Jenny.

"Yes. Hear that stream babbling down below? That goes through the small canyon where we pothole."

They dropped into a hollow, thick with heather and bilberry shrubs.

"What's that? One of your potholes?" Jenny pointed to a rocky opening which was boarded up half-way.

"No. There used to be lead-mining here. The old shafts are covered over with piles of rocks to stop any animal or man falling in. That was a long cavern cut by miners, or maybe it was natural. Anyway, trucks with ore travelled on narrow rails through it to the old road."

"If we had a torch I'd like to go in," said Jenny. "Those boards don't look very tough. I bet we could move them."

"I always carry a torch," said Alun. "Potholing habit, I suppose. But Auntie Beti wouldn't like it a bit, you know. There could be a rock-fall blocking the old tunnel."

"And the rocks could fall with us inside," mocked Jenny. "Come on. You're a potholer, so you can't be scared."

"Potholing has taught me to be careful, and not foolhardy," replied Alun with a sudden dignity. "We'll try it. But if it's dodgy, out we get, and no argument."

"Aye, aye, skipper," grinned Jenny.

The boards came apart easily.

"Queer!" said Alun thoughtfully. "Somebody's moved these; they used to be a tight fit."

Once inside, Alun shone his torch on the roof,

along the rocky sides, and then on to the narrow railway track. Jenny's eyes followed the light. But she made no move to go on, just stood sniffing.

"Alun, what's that queer smell? An oily, stuffy smell."

"Musty, I expect you mean." Alun was interested in the rocks, not the air.

But Jenny persisted. "No, not musty. It's like the smell of a woollen jersey when it's wet."

Slowly they moved on.

"Wet and muddy," remarked Jenny.

Alun shone the torch downwards and Jenny looked down at the rails, buried in mud.

"Alun," she said quietly. "I'm only a townee — but are those tiny hoof marks, or am I imagining things?"

Exclaiming, Alun crouched over the mud. Then he whispered, "If you think they are sheep hoofprints, you're dead right."

"So that's how it was done! No wonder I smelt oily, wet wool," exclaimed Jenny. "Your grandfather's sheep went by underground. Look! On that rock there's a wisp of sheep's wool."

Stunned, Alun said nothing.

"Where does this hole in the ground come out?" asked Jenny, hot on the trail.

"On the old road," replied Alun. "It's not used since the new shorter road was built. No houses, so no witnesses. It's full of potholes, but a lorry or horse-box, or a convoy of them, could take it."

"We'll go back and report it," he decided, taking Jenny by the arm.

"There's no hurry now," said Jenny. "We're weeks late. Let's follow through."

Silently they went on, following the trail of tiny hoof-prints. Suddenly, Alun stopped.

"Look, Jenny. There's a rock fall ahead. Near the tunnel mouth, I think. I can see daylight beyond."

Jenny squinted. "It's a boulder. Maybe we could crawl through the side gap. We're both skinny."

"And bring down some more," warned Alun.

"Hush! I thought I heard a groan. Let's look," said Jenny fearfully.

"There are always strange noises underground," said Alun. "But if you must look, come on. Move lightly and keep quiet."

Carefully they tiptoed towards the rock fall. Occasionally, Alun stopped Jenny while he examined the roof ahead of them. At last they reached the rock-slip. The torch light, helped by the faint daylight, showed an outstretched arm.

Jenny whimpered quietly.

"Stay here. I'll get through the gap," Alun gulped, "and look."

Alone, Jenny felt strangely calm, staring at the outline of an arm, faintly visible in the twilight of the tunnel mouth. It seemed hours, but it was actually only minutes before Alun shone the torch through the gap.

"It's O.K.," he whispered. "He's unconscious, but breathing. Can you come?"

Helped by Alun, Jenny squeezed through the gap. Gripping her arm hard, he shone the light on the figure of a man trapped by the boulder lying across his legs. Bracing herself, Jenny looked at the man — the little red-haired man.

"So . . ." she began.

"He wasn't in Shropshire, you were right," whispered Alun. He hesitated. Then he said, "Somebody's got to stay with him, and somebody's got to get help — whatever he's done."

Jenny swallowed nervously. "I'll stay. You know the quickest way to get help."

"Have my torch, and watch the roof. If the earth starts coming down or anything, you must run. Promise me, Jenny."

"I promise."

Never had Jenny felt so alone. The presence of the little man increased her feeling of loneliness. She kept telling herself that men don't die from broken legs. But why was he so silent?

Then he groaned, and muttered, "Butch, is that you, Butch?"

"Not Butch," said Jenny hoarsely, and somewhere an echo caught the words and threw back "Butch". "Help's coming," said Jenny, feeling braver at the sound of her own voice.

But the man had passed out again.

There was a rustling sound in the roof and,

remembering Alun's warning of the danger of more rock falls, Jenny shone the light upwards. Clinging to the roof was a family of bats. Jenny remembered reading that bats have an inborn instinct for danger. If there was any risk surely they would flit elsewhere.

An hour passed before Jenny heard the sound of footsteps on the rock outside. Her ordeal was over.

"Alright, Jenny?" cried Alun, as he entered, followed by Evans the Police and five other men.

"Fine," said Jenny.

A man stepped forward.

"I'm a doctor. Has he been conscious at all?"

"He spoke once," replied Jenny. "But I don't think he was properly conscious."

"What did he say?" rapped Evans the Police.

"Butch."

"Butch — short for butcher," said the policeman importantly.

"This is no time for an official inquiry," said the doctor. "Men, see what can be done to free him. Alun will take you home, Jenny. You've had enough."

Outside, Alun said, "I came as quickly as I could." Then, noticing Jenny shaking, he asked, "Shall I beg a lift from the Panda car on the old road?"

"No, thanks. Let's walk," replied Jenny. "The air's so good and fresh."

"What will happen to him?" asked Jenny, after they had gone a little way.

"If he's alive when they free him he'll go to hospital, and then the law will take over," replied Alun soberly.

Jenny had been home in the Midlands for two months, and the solving of the mystery of the Welsh hills had become a memory, when Alun sent her the cutting from a local paper. The little bandy-legged man had been the top rustler, and had to limp his way through some years of prison life.

"Grandfather had compensation for his sheep," wrote Alun, "and they've blasted the old tunnel. It's just fallen rubble now."

"I wonder what happened to the bats?" murmured Jenny.

THE GHOST OF AMY ROBSART

The end of the Summer Term was fast approaching, and as a special treat Miss Greenhalgh had promised the girls of St Clements an outing.

All sorts of suggestions had been put up, but the one which received most interest was one made by Wanda Hendrix and her friend Lois Blakeney. They had conceived the idea of a visit to Butterworth Manor after reading about it in a guide-book they had stumbled across in the library after school.

In actual fact it was Wanda who had told Lois about it. She had been doing some research for a history essay and had gone to the library one Wednesday evening. History was Wanda's favourite subject and it was no surprise for Lois to come across her avidly reading in the library every historical document she could lay her hands on.

"Oh, come on, Wanda," she had said after a while, "I must get back. I've got my English prep to do."

"Just a tick," Wanda said. "I think I've found something."

"What is it this time?" Lois asked with a touch

of impatience. She had never liked history, and Wanda's fanatical interest irritated her.

"You know the story of Amy Robsart," Wanda said.

"Which story?" Lois probed. "You mean the Cumnor affair?"

"Yes, that's right," Wanda said. "Well, I've just come across a Manor House she was reputed to have stayed at frequently before that ghastly episode resulting in her death. It's called Butterworth. Look, there's a picture of it here," she said, eagerly thrusting a book under Lois' nose.

Lois stared at the picture for a few seconds. Butterworth Manor was a huge, Gothic building and she could just imagine the interior; cold, dank and musty-smelling rooms which hadn't been used for years. It probably housed a few ghosts as well, she thought with distaste.

She returned the book to Wanda, saying as she did so, "Well, what about it?"

"Why don't we suggest to Miss Greenhalgh we'd like to visit Butterworth for our end-of-term outing?"

"You must be mad," Lois declared. "No one would want to visit a place like that."

"How do you know until we ask?" Wanda persisted.

The next morning Wanda asked the girls in her form about her proposal to visit Butterworth.

"Has it got ghosts?" Lindsay Kerr asked, giggling.

"I bet it has, a place like that," Gilly said with great mirth. "Those places usually have. Who wants to see ghosts anyway? I'd much rather go to Harmondsworth Castle."

"Anyway, ghosts aren't supposed to appear until dusk, are they?" Marella pointed out. "And we shan't be there then, so what's the point of going? I certainly don't want a conducted tour of a gloomy old Manor."

"You're all being silly," Wanda said quietly. "Butterworth has great historic significance. Amy Robsart is supposed to have stayed there."

"Who's Amy Robsart?" tittered Penny Walters.

"Queen Elizabeth's rival, idiot," someone said.

"I agree with Gilly," Penny persisted. "Give me a castle any day."

"A castle's likely to be just as gloomy," Wanda said. "Even gloomier, I'll bet."

"Does it *have* to be a place of historic interest?" Lindsay asked. "Couldn't we go to the beach?"

"Can you imagine Miss Greenhalgh agreeing to that?" Lois pointed out. "It's obviously got to be somewhere historic, because she teaches history."

"Well, what about Hampton Court then, or Windsor Castle?"

"Too popular, and anyway we've all been there."

"I think Butterworth's a good idea," Betsy Anderson piped up. "Anyway no one has come up with a better suggestion yet."

"We haven't been given a chance," Penny groaned. "And anyway, Wanda always gets her way with Miss Greenhalgh, so I suppose it is bound to be Butterworth, despite our feelings."

"Not if you vote unanimously for something else," Wanda pointed out.

But in the end, when Miss Greenhalgh put it to the vote, the verdict was predictably Butterworth, and even Lois had come round to thinking quite favourably about the idea.

That evening in the library Wanda said, "I've been reading about Butterworth. It seems there is a secret passage from which Amy Robsart was smuggled out when her life was in danger from Queen Elizabeth. I don't know where it leads or how we shall find it, but find it I will. I'm determined to do that. Also," she said mysteriously, "it appears Butterworth *is* haunted."

"Oh no," Lois groaned. "I'm terrified of ghosts."

"This one's a friendly ghost," Wanda explained. "In fact stories about it differ, but rumour has it that it is the anguished ghost of Amy Robsart."

By this time Lois's eyes were bulging with suppressed excitement. "Go on," she said, eager for Wanda to continue. "But why should she haunt a place like Butterworth?"

"Because according to the stories the owner of Butterworth, Sir Glenville Pike, a staunch supporter of Queen Elizabeth I, offered to help Amy

Robsart flee the Queen's wrath and go with Robert Dudley to Cumnor, by allowing her to stay at Butterworth Manor.

"In fact he betrayed her, and held her hostage. But she managed to escape. You know the rest. Some time later she met a tragic death in Cumnor. After that she came back, smarting to revenge herself on Sir Glenville Pike.

"The story goes that she appeared on the night of the full moon. She was such a piteous ghost that Sir Glenville Pike was stricken with guilt for what he had done and he fled from Butterworth and the ghost of Amy Robsart. His son moved in soon after, but he was driven out in similar fashion. Since then it has remained curiously empty, except for a period when a family called Marchbanks attempted to live there but, one by one, they too moved away.

"Butterworth proved too large and too expensive to support, but as far as I know Amy Robsart did not appear to them, and has not done so since she haunted Sir Glenville's son, Charles. That is why I am so keen on the idea of visiting the Manor. I want to see if Amy will come back."

"But how will she do that?" Lois asked incredulously. "That is if she has not appeared for over two hundred years?"

"They say if a ghost senses a sympathetic atmosphere, he or she will appear."

"Yes, but her sole purpose in haunting Butterworth was surely to drive Sir Glenville Pike and all his ancestors away?" Lois said. "And now they have gone, why should she have cause to return?"

"Because I think she is still in agony and cannot forget the heinous crime that led to her betrayal. I have a feeling in my bones she will come back. I've been reading and thinking a lot about her and somehow I feel that there was something in her past life that prevented her from finding eternal peace. I can't believe she just came out of hatred for Sir Glenville."

"Then why did she return?" Lois asked. "And anyway how shall we get rid of Penny, Gilly and the rest of the form, especially Miss Greenhalgh? You know how she always sticks to you just because you're so good at history."

"We'll manage it, don't worry," Wanda said. "With so many girls we can easily slip away, and it will be ages before they discover us. Anyway I know the exact location where Amy is said to appear. She is supposed to walk along the secret passage and climb the stairs to Sir Glenville's bedchamber. So all we've got to do is find the secret passage."

"Yes, but you said yourself you don't know where it is, nor how to find it. Butterworth looks a huge place to me from the pictures. It could take us all day."

"I shouldn't," Wanda said, "not if we use our heads. I've taken a tracing from a map of Butterworth I found in the library book I showed you. I have a hunch it will be in the West Wing. In fact I've marked four likely spots on the map. All we have to do is to give Miss Greenhalgh and the girls the slip. But for goodness sake don't breathe a word to anyone."

"Trust me," Lois said. "I'm as anxious as you are to see Amy Robsart's ghost, as long as she's friendly, that is."

At last the day dawned for the excursion. It was a fine, warm day and Penny Walters was the first in the school bus, racing to bag the back seat with all her chums, Gilly, Susannah, Blondie and Carla.

Wanda and Lois found a seat together, while Miss Greenhalgh chatted to Lindsay Kerr, much to Lindsay's chagrin.

Wanda had the map of Butterworth in her blazer pocket, ready to use at the first opportunity.

They reached Butterworth soon after eleven o'clock and, to their surprise, Miss Greenhalgh said that instead of a conducted tour she would allow the girls to explore the Manor on their own provided they were careful, behaved properly and took care to be ready for the bus at four o'clock that afternoon. When they had seen the Manor they could eat their picnic lunch in the grounds. But they must be sure to behave themselves and not leave litter strewn about.

"Now, remember, girls," she warned, "the hon-

our of St Clements is at stake. So see you act accordingly."

The next instant the girls were scattering in all directions, leaving Miss Greenhalgh to make arrangements for departure with the driver.

Penny and her chums had dashed straight to the East wing, while Lindsay, glad to be rid of the history mistress, teamed up with a crowd strolling the Great Hall.

"Come on," Wanda whispered to Lois. "Quick, while no one's looking."

So straightaway they headed for the West Wing.

"The staircase is bound to be on the ground floor, or more likely the basement, if we can reach it," Wanda whispered. "It probably begins in a Priest's Hole. You know, the concealed hideaways they used to hide priests in during the Reformation. Usually they are situated beside fireplaces, so keep a sharp look out. Also, if you come across any panelling, look hard for any possible openings. For instance, if the wood sounds hollow . . ."

"I know . . ." Lois interjected.

"We'll search the ground floor first, shall we, trying all the hearths?"

"Lead on," Lois encouraged.

Doing as Wanda instructed, they searched hearth after hearth with no success. The rooms were high and musty as if no air had penetrated for centuries.

"That'll be our first clue, if we smell oxygen,"

Wanda said. "It'll be easily detectable in this atmosphere."

"Yes, if we could find it," Lois answered dejectedly. "We've been here for hours already. I've made my fingers sore tapping at the panelling."

"Well, we'll try the basement," Wanda said, studying the map as she descended the winding stairs. "And if that's hopeless, there's only one place left, and that's Sir Glenville Pike's bedchamber."

"Penny and her chums are bound to be there," Lois said.

"We'll just have to dodge them, then," Wanda replied with determination.

Lois could see that nothing would distract Wanda from her search, so obediently she followed down the stairs. The basement proved no more revealing than the ground floor and, despondently, they had to admit defeat.

"Come on," Wanda said, "I've just remembered something. Amy's ghost never appeared until the afternoon, so we wouldn't see her now even if we *did* discover the passage. Why don't we get some fresh air, eat our lunch and search Sir Glenville's bedchamber later?"

"Good idea," Lois agreed.

It was wonderful to breathe the fresh air again. They found a large, shady tree and, with their backs to the trunk, they opened their food parcels and tucked into their lunch.

Munching an apple, Lois said, "Funny . . . the others seem to have disappeared."

"That's good," Wanda remarked. "We don't want them asking questions at this stage. I'm going to take another look at the map," she said, spreading it out in front of her on the grass.

"Yes, look, here's Sir Grenville's bedchamber," she said, tracing the position of the West Wing with her finger.

"By jove, I think I've got it, Lois," she suddenly yelled. "The panelling in this room probably conceals the hidden staircase. This is the place from which he promised Amy she would escape. Amy Robsart came to Butterworth, saw the passage and really believed Sir Glenville meant to help her, so she went to her room and spent a peaceful night, never dreaming he meant to betray her. Perhaps that afternoon — it would be foggy, maybe almost dark for it was a December day — she entered the passage and was intercepted by Queen Elizabeth's troops. That is why she still chooses to use this passage to make her appearance. This was where she was betrayed."

"Gosh, I think you're right," Lois said, scrambling to her feet. "There isn't a moment to be lost. Come on," she yelled, and with that she took to her heels and fled across the grass, with Wanda for once behind her.

They clattered up the staircase of the West Wing, regardless of whether or not Penny and her chums were there. But they encountered no one.

Panting hard, they reached Sir Glenville's bedchamber, swung shut the massive oak door, and shot the bolt.

Lois looked at her watch. It was exactly half past two.

"Start searching," she ordered Wanda to her surprise, and dutifully Wanda did as she was told.

They tapped piece by piece the panelling of the bedchamber.

"Oh help, we'll never find it," Wanda said, collapsing on to Sir Glenville's bed with fatigue and disappointment. "We've been round the entire room. There's only one thing left. We'll just have to wait and see."

"If only I could smell fresh air, or find some clue," Lois was saying, when suddenly Wanda sat bolt upright on the bed. "Listen," she commanded earnestly. "Do you hear that?"

"Oh, that . . . that's Penny and her chums down below on the lawn."

"*Shuuuuush!*" Wanda hissed. "It's someone walking. Footsteps. Listen. Do you hear them now?"

Lois listened. Sure enough there came the sound of slow footsteps, but they were not the heavy, shuffling footfalls usually connected with ghosts, but light, almost carefree sounds, as if someone were fleeing from Butterworth with a joyful heart on her way to her reunion with her husband, Robert Dudley, Earl of Leicester.

"It's her," Wanda hissed. "But is she coming this way or going away from us?"

"She's coming this way," Lois said with conviction. "The footsteps are getting louder. But why is the step so gay?"

"Because she trusted Sir Glenville and thought he meant to lead her to Dudley."

"So she rushed to her own destruction."

"Ultimately, yes," Wanda said quietly.

Both girls were listening hard. The footsteps were certainly getting nearer and the step was still light and free, but from which direction was the sound coming?

Then, all at once, a draught of fresh air rushed into the room.

Lois glanced around her. All the windows were closed, so it could mean only one thing.

"Quick, over to the fireplace," Wanda hissed.

Sure enough as they rested their backs against the panelling of the hearth they heard the footsteps quite distinctly.

Momentarily they stopped, as if the person to whom they belonged had had second thoughts, a moment's hesitation before continuing her journey, and then they started again, this time with ever-increasing proximity.

In a flash the panelling on the opposite side of the fireplace to that behind which Lois and Wanda were leaning started to slide open. They clapped their hands over their mouths to stifle their gasps of astonishment.

192

Into the bedchamber of Sir Glenville Pike had stepped a fair young woman, golden curls falling nonchalantly down her back. Her cloak, of rich, ruby-coloured velvet, was drawn closely over her thin, youthful body. The hood, thrown back, revealed the lovely face and candid blue eyes of a young girl waiting for the reunion with the Earl of Leicester.

She moved quickly towards the bed with its gold embroidered coverlet and she began to search in a gold embossed cabinet by the bedside.

She seemed bent on discovering some old and musty secret. So feverish was her activity, so great her haste, that it was almost as if the troops were at the door, as they had been that fateful December afternoon with an English mist settling beyond the windows.

She gave little gasps as she rushed hither and thither in the bedchamber, opening boxes, but never finding what she was looking for.

There were so many questions Lois wanted to ask, but she dared not open her mouth in case she frightened the young woman away.

Together they watched, mesmerised, as Amy Robsart continued her search. And then, with a small girlish cry, she clasped in her hands a jewelled box, its lid encrusted with sapphires, emeralds, amethysts and rubies. Opening it, she gently extracted a ring and held it up to the light, her face breaking into a soft smile of contentment.

Wanda and Lois held their breath.

The ring, far from being of the type and opulence they expected was a simple, gold band, but entwined at its centre were two gold pieces twisted into a lovers' knot.

At long last Amy had found what she was looking for at Butterworth Manor. With a small ecstatic cry she crossed the room to where the panelled door was open for her to walk through. With a light step, Amy crossed the threshold to the secret passage, and the door slid shut behind her.

For an instant Wanda and Lois held their breath as the footsteps began slowly to get more and more distant, until there was no sound in the room except the pounding of their hearts.

Wanda was the first to speak.

"Oh, I'm so glad she found it, Lois," she breathed. "That was what she had been searching for all this time. The ring, given to her by Robert Dudley and taken from her by Sir Glenville Pike."

"I wonder, though, why she stopped searching after Sir Glenville's departure from Butterworth?" Lois asked.

"Because she knew the ring was confiscated by Sir Glenville and his family and still remained in their possession, forever out of reach. You see, the house has recently been restored and all its original furniture returned."

"Then why did she choose to reveal herself today, after long centuries had passed?"

"That I can't answer," Wanda said. "I can only assume there is some truth in the supposition that if ghosts sense a sympathetic atmosphere they will reveal themselves."

"Poor Amy Robsart!" Lois sighed.

"She is happy now," Wanda said confidently. "She has found what she has been looking for all these long years. She has been reunited."

For a moment they stood there, unable to believe they were standing in the twentieth century in Sir Glenville Pike's bedchamber, scene of one of the most notorious betrayals of the Tudor Age.

"At least we don't have to worry about Amy Robsart any more. But what became of Sir Glenville Pike?" Lois wanted to know.

"He's buried in a pauper's grave in a remote cemetery in the Hebrides," Wanda explained. "After the haunting, he became quite demented and the nobles snatched all his silver, jewels and possessions, leaving him with nothing."

"Despite that, I can't feel sorry for him," Lois said, "not when I think how poor Amy suffered."

"Neither can I," Wanda said stoutly. "But at least we've solved the mystery. I'm so very glad about that."

"Me, too," Lois agreed. "I'm so pleased you suggested Butterworth Manor, Wanda. Just imagine what we'd have missed if you hadn't."

Wanda merely smiled as they descended the staircase of the West Wing and found themselves once again on the broad, sweeping lawns of Butterworth Manor.

"Where have you two been?" asked Lindsay.

"Oh, just looking back at some history," Wanda replied and she smiled at Lois. It was their secret, and who would believe it anyway?

THE HAT-TRICK HOLIDAY

"Well, here we are!"

"I wish the butterflies inside me would go away!"

Penny and Sue jumped out of their seats as the train slid into the country station, quickly gathering up their suitcases and bags.

"Can you see anyone to meet us?" Penny asked, gazing anxiously out of the window. Sue shook her head and was about to speak when the train came to a noisy halt at Platform 1.

"This is it!" The two girls were almost the only passengers to leave the train. They stood on the platform while the train sped off once more. Everywhere was quiet and still.

"Just smell that air! Isn't it fresh!" Penny, a city girl born and bred, sniffed appreciatively. But Sue was more worried about whether they would be met. She dumped her luggage, and her precious guitar case, down on a bench and went over to the Ticket Office. It was deserted.

But just at that moment a man rushed through the entrance and looked around. Catching Penny's eye, he hurried towards her with a smile. Penny decided she liked the look of this rugged farmer in muddy wellingtons and wind-swept, greying hair.

"Hello!" the man said. "You're not the Millingtons, are you?"

"Yes, I'm Penny, and that's Sue," she replied, pointing at her sister, who was approaching.

"Glad to meet you!" He turned to pick up the cases. "I'm Mr Radley, from the farm. Sorry I was late, but I had some things to collect in the village and I was held up. Just follow me!"

The journey to the farm was spent in a battered Landrover, with Penny and Sue squeezed in beside various sacks of feed and sharp edged implements neither girl could guess the uses of. But Mr Radley was such a friendly man that they soon lost their nervousness and were chatting away happily.

"I hope you'll find it interesting with us," Mr Radley was saying. "We work hard, but then you'll have some idea of what to expect, if you're wanting to go to college in the autumn. What was it you said you were studying, exactly?"

"Well, I'm going to take a course in agriculture, and Penny is doing a secretarial course — she wants to be an agricultural secretary and later handle accounts and things like that for big farms and estates," Sue told him.

"Good! Good!" Mr Radley laughed as he turned

down a lane off the road and the Landrover heaved and rolled over great ruts in the mud. "I'm always glad to hear of young people who want to come into farming. It's a great life!"

Penny, her face a strange colour, was digging her sister in the ribs. Sue merely smiled, and ignored her. Soon they drew up in front of a white-painted farmhouse. A woman was standing in the doorway, waving.

"How do you do," she said, when she was introduced. "I'm Mrs Radley. Now I'll just show you your room, then when you've had a bit of a wash, we'll have some dinner."

The room they were to share was glorious. Nestling beneath the eaves, it looked out over soft green countryside to distant blue hills. But neither girl seemed interested; the minute the door closed behind Mrs Radley, Penny turned to Sue.

"What on earth were you going on about, back there?" she demanded. "You're going to the College of Music next term and it's true I'm going to train to be a secretary, but all that agricultural stuff is rubbish — I plan to get a very comfortable, very well-paid job in the middle of the city!"

Sue lay back on one of the neatly made beds and grinned. "I should have told you, I suppose," she admitted. "But when I answered the ad. Mr Radley just assumed we knew a bit about working on a farm and so I just kidded him on a little bit. We wouldn't have got the job otherwise, you know that!"

Penny sighed. "Oh, Sue! I wish you'd told me! I don't want to stay here by having to tell lies! Anyway, as soon as we begin work it'll be terribly obvious we don't know anything about farms at all!"

"Not really. There's nothing to it — we'll be given all the easy things, like forking hay and cleaning out stables."

"I hope you're right. I don't know why you're always so devious about everything, Sue, I really don't."

Sue only smiled. She had her own reasons, but Penny wouldn't find them out — yet . . .

Mr Radley had been right when he had said the work would be hard. Up at six each morning, by the time it was dark the two girls felt every muscle aching. There were countless small tasks to be done, and redone the next day. But the sun shone, and both of them enjoyed themselves.

Penny, who adored animals, fell in love with some of the occupants of the farmyard: the new kittens, an enormous glistening pig, and some of the chestnut horses they had to groom. It was a small farm but a busy one, and there were other farm workers to make friends with. Geordie was one, a bright, cheerful young man who lived in one of the farm cottages with his family. There was a happy atmosphere everywhere, which helped ease the sisters' tiredness.

Soon after their arrival, Penny was helping Mrs Radley with baking some bread — a job she had never done before. It was fun, in the warm kitchen, to knead the dough and chat with the farmer's wife, a kind and open-hearted woman.

"Are you settling all right?" she asked Penny. "I often think it takes a while for someone from the city to get used to our ways."

"Oh, we're both having a great time!" Penny smiled.

Mrs Radley looked curiously at her. "Forgive my asking," she began, "but it does seem a little strange that two girls from the city should be so interested in farming. What made you and your sister want to take it up as a career?"

"Oh, er, well, we had an — an uncle who owned a farm, and that's where we got the inspiration," Penny stammered, cursing her sister inwardly.

All these lies just for a holiday in the country with a bit of work and some pocket money thrown in! It had been Sue who had persuaded her to come in the first place and made all the arrangements. Penny, although she liked the Radleys and the farm, was beginning to wish she had gone on holiday with her parents to Cornwall instead.

"Well, it seemed a godsend when your sister answered our advert," Mrs Radley said. "We've had all sorts of flibberty-gibberts in the past —

people who don't even think to close a gate. So when Sue told us you were serious about farming, we breathed a sigh of relief!"

Sue had begged a morning off from Mr Radley, and without a word to Penny, had slipped up to her room. Collecting her guitar, she had managed to walk up the road towards the village with no one being the wiser.

It was quite a long way to the village, but Sue's heart was beating so quickly she hoped the brisk walk would calm her down. Hardly noticing the lovely countryside around her, her thoughts strayed again and again to a newspaper article which was folded carefully in her jeans pocket. It said:

WORLD FAMOUS GUITARIST BUYS HIDEAWAY COTTAGE.

Below the headline the print was faded with continual fingering, and the paper torn around the folds. But Sue knew the rest of the article by heart.

Reaching the village, she went into the Post Office.

"Can you tell me where Applemere Cottage is, please?"

"Go down to the river and over the bridge. Then follow the lane to its end and there'll be a sign to turn left. It's about a mile." The Post Mistress eyed the young girl curiously. "Aren't you that girl who's working with the Radleys?" she asked. But with a wave, and a jingle of the bell, Sue had closed the door.

"Where's Sue?" Penny asked Geordie that afternoon. They were feeding the pigs, a job Sue usually did, although it wasn't either sister's favourite job.

Geordie shook his head. "Mr Radley said she asked for a morning off, but he was expecting her back before lunch."

"Wasn't she at lunch?" Penny asked, with mounting disquiet. She had been out in one of the farther fields and had taken sandwiches, so she hadn't gone to the farmhouse.

"No!" Geordie laughed. "It's my bet she's gone back home!"

"What do you mean?"

"Oh, you could tell at a glance she wasn't cut out for this work. Look at her hands! And since you two came she's left you with the lion's share of the work to do! I shouldn't be surprised if she's given up and gone home!"

"Sue wouldn't do that!" Penny said, stung.

Geordie laughed again, flinging his curly hair from his face and smiling at her with blue eyes. "City folk!" he grinned.

Penny was furious. "I'm working hard enough, aren't I? Are you saying that we're useless?"

Geordie's smile faded. "I'm not saying *you're*

useless," he replied. "But beat me if you or your sister have much idea about farmwork!"

Penny sighed. "I suppose Mr Radley told you we were going to get involved with farming careers, did he? Well, I'm tired of making excuses — Sue made all that up. She wants to be a musician and I want to be a secretary. We've only been to the country on day trips and you're right, we don't know anything about farming. Now I expect Mr Radley will send us home."

Geordie looked at Penny thoughtfully. "Are you enjoying yourself here?"

"Oh, yes! I love it much more than I thought I would!"

"Well, I don't think your sister's stories make any difference, then, do you? I'm glad you came, Penny."

Penny was suddenly glad she had come, too.

Applemere Cottage was set far back from the lane, hidden by high hedges and trees. Its walls shone sparkling white and roses framed the door. Sue walked up the path with bated breath, and knocked on the door.

It was a long time before the door opened. A middle-aged man with a shock of white hair and a gentle face stood in the shadows. He was wearing old, worn clothes and holding a book.

"Yes?"

Sue took all her courage into her hands. "My name is Sue Millington, Mr Lopez. I've come a long way to talk to you. Will you let me come in?"

Mr Lopez was about to close the door with a gesture of annoyance when he noticed Sue's tightly-held guitar case. A faint smile brushed over his face.

"Ah, my child, you play the guitar," he said. "Yes, you may come in and see me. I have all the time in the world." His face was very sad as he stood back to let Sue walk in.

The cottage was pleasant but untidy. Sue sat in the living room in a chintz armchair while the world-famous musician made tea. Then they sat in the sunlight of the garden.

"Why did you come?" he asked. "It seems everyone else in the world has forgotten me since the accident. I took this cottage to forget what has happened — and it seems I, in return, have been forgotten."

"I read about the cottage in the paper," Sue said, taking out her tattered piece of print. "I have bought all the recordings you ever made — and I was determined to play as well as you, if I could, some day. It seemed so wrong, somehow, when you gave up playing. So when I knew you were coming to this country I made up my mind to see you."

Rudy Lopez smiled. "You are so young," he said, "but so determined. Some day, I think, you will be famous, too."

"Do you — do you still play the guitar?" Sue asked.

"Very little. I have lost my touch. Since the accident I have shaking in my hands. And I am not so young." He buried his head in his hands. Sue was overcome with pity by the sight of the world's greatest guitar player reduced to such dejection.

She reached over and said: "The reason I came was because I wanted to ask you if you would play for me. Will you?"

Mr Lopez looked up. "I would prefer it if *you* played for *me*. Open your guitar case and begin."

Sue did as he said, and nervously began to play. At first her fingers trembled over the frets, but the peace of the sunlit garden relaxed her and by the close of the piece she had played better than ever before.

"Aah!" Mr Lopez opened his eyes and smiled. "I was right, you *will* go far some day. You have real feeling for the music that you play. Hearing that piece takes me back to my first years . . ."

"Play for me now, Mr Lopez," Sue begged. "I know you can do it! All you need is your old confidence!"

Without a word Rudy Lopez disappeared into the cottage and returned with his guitar of gleaming wood. In silence he sat down with it and haltingly began to play. In the still air the melody rose as sweet as birdsong. Sue sat spellbound, her whole life suspended.

At the end of the music, the old man and the

young girl sat quite quiet, looking at each other. Then Mr Lopez began to smile. . . .

The train was almost empty when it pulled into the station, and there were few people waiting on the platform: just a homely, farming couple, a good-looking young man with windswept hair and a dignified old man with white hair, waving goodbye to two girls who were boarding the train.

At last the train was on its way, and the two girls were alone in the compartment

"Well!" commented Penny. "Back to real life! What a great holiday that was!" She grinned at her sister. "I've got you to thank for fixing it up — even if you did have reasons of your own!"

Sue smiled. "Yes, everything turned out really well — you've been invited back to the Radleys' anytime, and Geordie's going to start writing to you . . . while me — " She closed her eyes in delight. "I'm now a personal friend and protégé of the great Rudy Lopez!"

"And you helped him get back on his feet after that awful car accident," Penny added. "You are awfully devious, Sue, but I have to admit this time you really pulled off a hat trick!"

And the two girls went on chattering happily as the train sped on through the countryside on its way home to the city.

SKY BABY

Val Kerry — better known as Valkyrie — dived her light aircraft a few feet over the vineyard and switched on the insecticide spray. She flew a straight course to deposit an even layer, then she switched off the spray, climbed away smoothly to give her enough height to bank safely, and turned and dived to spray the next lane.

"I'll take control now," said the pilot. "There's a rising in the corner of the vineyard which is deceptive. We can't take any chances."

"But I can manage," protested Valkyrie.

"Don't argue, Valkyrie. That's rule number one in the air."

As the captain piloted the aircraft, Valkyrie sank back in her co-pilot's seat and pouted her lips. Although she was a qualified pilot, the captain made it quite obvious that he did not trust her to fly in anything but the most ideal conditions. Even then he only allowed her to use the co-pilot's seat. He would watch every move she made, with his hands hovering over the joystick, ready to snatch control at the slightest opportunity.

Valkyrie sat back and fumed. She gazed out over the rich countryside of Idaho, and beyond, to the snow-capped Rocky Mountains. The scenery was magnificent.

Valkyrie ought to have been the happiest girl in the world, instead she was the most miserable. She could not feel otherwise, for the captain constantly made her feel inferior and useless as a pilot.

The captain happily finished off the spraying operation and landed beside the second charter spray aircraft just in front of the ranch-house. He switched off his ignition and hopped out of his aircraft. He looked over the vast vineyard, now covered in a haze of white powder.

"We've made a good start today, Valkyrie," he said over his shoulder. "I reckon we've sprayed over ten square miles of vineyards this morning, and that's not bad, by any standard."

Valkyrie was not so happy. She turned on her captain as soon as she stepped out of the aircraft.

"Why didn't you let me finish the job properly? Remember I'm a qualified pilot too, or have you forgotten? Every time I settle down to a spraying job, you have to take over. . . ."

"But Val, you are still new to this game. It wouldn't be right for me to let you take chances. You haven't got the experience. . . ."

"And how do you expect me to get the experience with you looking over my shoulder all the time? Why don't you let me sort out my own problems for a change?"

"But Val, I only take over when there's any danger."

"Flying *isn't* dangerous, and I regard myself as a

pretty safe pilot at any time. You don't treat Andy, your other pilot, like that. It isn't fair. You won't even let me fly the aircraft solo on a simple cross-country flight from farm to farm, and there's nothing dangerous in that. What's the matter? Don't you trust me at all?"

The captain sighed. "All right, all right, all right. I'll fly with Andy across the Rockies to our next client's farm. You can fly solo. As there is no low flying involved, I think even you will be safe enough."

Valkyrie almost exploded. "Even me? Safe enough? Oh!"

But the captain wasn't listening. Already he had walked across to the other charter aircraft.

Valkyrie was almost speechless, but she choked back her frustration and went off to pick up a can of fuel. The captain did not help her, which was a consolation, for had he told her once again how to refuel her aircraft she would have resigned on the spot and found herself another flying job.

The two light aircraft flew off to cross the Rocky Mountains. Valkyrie was a little happier now, for at least she was flying solo, and there was no one beside her to constantly tell her what to do. She knew happy-go-lucky Andy was piloting the leading aircraft by the determined way he flew. She watched him veer off his pre-planned route to have a closer look at a couple of mountain eagles soaring over the mountain valley, and she wished her captain had the same confidence in her as he had in Andy.

Andy flew too close to the eagles, and one of them, with a six-foot wing span, thinking it was about to be attacked by the man-made bird, flicked over on one wing and dived at the aircraft.

Valkyrie almost felt the thud as the eagle ran into the propeller. Miraculously the aircraft flew on with its motor still running, but now there was nothing to be seen of the attacking eagle.

"Mayday, mayday, emergency, emergency!" yelled Andy over his radio. "I'm flying blind. I've just collided with a bird and its body and feathers have splattered my windscreen."

Valkyrie dived on to the scene and switched on her spray to frighten away the eagle's mate which was still orbiting menacingly. As soon as the eagle ran into the spray cloud it heeled over and climbed away rapidly to its home in the mountain tops.

"How . . . how are you now, Andy?" called Valkyrie.

"I'm flying blind," came the voice over the radio. "I . . . I can see out of my side window, but the front windscreen is completely covered up."

"No engine trouble?"

"No engine trouble, but that's not much consolation if I can't see where I'm going."

"Hang on, Andy," said Valkyrie. "I'll fly beside you and lead you through the mountains."

Valkyrie flew in formation with the blind aircraft so that Andy could see her through his small side panel, and she guided him between the towering peaks of the Rocky Mountains. This she managed without mishap, but they still had to face the problem of a blind landing at an unfamiliar airstrip.

"This is your captain speaking," she heard the voice in her headphones. "Listen, Valkyrie. After we cross the mountains, I want you to take us in formation to the airstrip and talk us down right to the touchdown point. Can you do that?"

"I'll . . . I'll try," said Valkyrie, not feeling at all confident now.

"Good girl!"

Valkyrie had navigated the two aircraft across the Rocky Mountains safely enough, but when she saw the tiny airstrip in the undulating countryside she could have wept. From the air it looked no bigger than a bowling alley, and she knew that the steep-sided mountains surrounding the tiny airstrip would make a safe approach out of the question. Alternatively, the blind pilots could bale out; but the loss of their aircraft would ruin the little charter company.

"I . . . I can't take you down," she cried. "It's . . . too dangerous."

"Try, Valkyrie, try!" called out her captain. "You must try!"

"No, no. I can't!"

What her captain was asking her to do was impossible. Valkyrie knew she had to find another way to help.

"Orbit your aircraft, Andy," she called. "You will be quite safe if you fly on instruments."

With that, Valkyrie broke formation and dived for the tiny airstrip.

"Where are you, Valkyrie?" called her captain. "Come back! Come back at once! Don't you realise we're flying blind?"

Valkyrie switched off her radio to keep the cries out of her ears. She landed on the tiny airstrip, and hurriedly filled up her insecticide tanks with water. She worked quickly, for she knew that after their long journey over the Rocky Mountains, Andy would only have a few minutes supply of fuel left.

As soon as her insecticide tanks were full she flung herself into the cockpit, took off again, and climbed up to join the little aircraft orbiting helplessly in the sky.

"Andy," called Valkyrie over her radio. "Listen carefully. When I give you the signal, I want you to fly straight and level. Do you understand?"

"What do you have in mind, Valkyrie?" came Andy's voice. "I . . . I haven't much fuel left."

"I haven't time to tell you, Andy. Just do as I say."

The captain broke in. "This is no time for your silly little games. Do as I instructed you at once, do you hear? This is an order, Valkyrie!"

"Shut up, shut up!" Valkyrie burst out. "I have

no time to argue either. Fly staight and level . . . now!"

"Guess I ain't got much choice," said Andy.

She saw the blind aircraft level out and fly on a steady course. Valkyrie could imagine what her captain was growling under his breath, but she put these thoughts out of her mind. With her fingers trembling, she positioned her aircraft over the blind aircraft and switched on her spray.

"What are you doing?" yelled Andy. "The entire windscreen and side windows are covered with greasy spray. We . . . we are now completely blind."

Valkyrie had not anticipated this disaster, but she tried again. Eventually the water came through the spray nozzles and showered her sister aircraft.

"Jeepers! I . . . I can see now," yelled Andy excitedly. "Well done, Valkyrie. Well done."

Valkyrie heaved a sigh of relief and broke away from the other aircraft. She could see Andy's windscreen wiper going.

"The airstrip is behind you, Andy."

"Thanks, Valkyrie, I'll buy you a box of chocolates for this."

"Make it flowers, Andy. I'm slimming."

Valkyrie orbited and saw Andy's aircraft turn back and land safely. She waited for him to clear the airstrip, but before he could do so her own engine coughed and spluttered. She had run out of fuel. Apart from controlling her aircraft in a gentle

glide, there was nothing she could do to re-start her engine.

However, Valkyrie's low-flying experience proved to be invaluable. She banked in the restricted air space and came in to make a safe dead-stick landing.

The captain and Andy helped her down from the aircraft. She needed their assistance, for when she saw the towering mountains on the airstrip approach, her legs felt like jelly.

Her captain smiled. "I had planned to say a few words to you about disobeying my instructions," he said sheepishly, "but now I have the opportunity, I must admit you used your initiative. In all my experience I have never been in such a dangerous situation. Very few pilots could have got us down alive, Valkyrie."

Valkyrie pulled herself together. "In that case you can hardly object to me flying my own crop-spraying aircraft in future."

The captain shrugged his shoulders. "I wouldn't dare stand in your way now, Valkyrie."

"Then perhaps you'll excuse me while I fill up my insecticide tanks. There are over thirty square miles of orange groves to be sprayed, and I am anxious to be on my way."

The captain waved his hand aloft. "The sky is all yours for the rest of the day, Valkyrie. Andy and I are off to find the best florist on this side of the Rockies."

PEBBLECAT

Vicky Casson cycled up the lane ·towards the stables, daydreaming about the advertisement she had seen in the paper for a pupil wanted at the Glossop stables. Val Glossop and her show jumpers were always in the news. She wondered whether to write and apply, then decided, with a sigh, that she wasn't a good enough rider.

A friendly whinney greeted her at Conway's Training Stables where she had worked since leaving school at Easter. It was very early, barely light, and the cold, wet mud splashed up from the road. She parked her cycle and opened the door of a loose box. Vicky glanced up at Pebblecat, a magnificent bay of some three years. He started forward with ears pricked back and snapping teeth as Jimmy, the head lad, came up behind her.

Luckily for Vicky, Jimmy caught the bay by the nostrils and mane, and forced him back as she bolted the door.

"Better leave him a bit," said Jimmy. "Carry on with the next box. We'll take him out later on a training rope."

It was the sight of Jimmy, Vicky felt sure, that had upset the horse. He was as nervous as a cat and nearly wild, and Jimmy had no time to humour him.

Yesterday he had stood quite still and given no trouble as she groomed him, taking special pride in his splendid coat, even lifting his hooves to be oiled and blacked, without much persuasion. For the hundredth time she wished they would leave Pebblecat to her care. She wasn't too experienced a rider, she knew, and Mr Conway, the Guv'nor, refused to put her up on the horse, which had to have a double bit to keep him under control.

But many a morning, during the ride, she had stayed behind and made his bed and been there to groom him on his return, watched by Susan, the Guv'nor's small daughter. Vicky had been warned to keep him tied up while grooming, and this she had done; but the last few mornings, she had slipped a halter on and removed the bridle, and he had been as good as gold.

Vicky carried on making horses' beds and began doing 'tack' until the lads returned with their mounts from the morning ride. She wondered if she would get a ride, later on. Sometimes she did, but if the Guv'nor was going away to a race, there wasn't a lot to do and the apprentices and stable lads drifted off about their own business. She was the only girl.

The lads unsaddled and led their horses into the stables, threw rugs over them and went across to the kitchen. "Tea up, Vicky," called Jimmy, as he

went by, and Vicky picked up her sandwiches and followed him. Her watch said nine-thirty.

Mick, the old Irishman employed about the place, walked beside her. "I'll put you up on something later," he promised. She liked Mick, who had worked with horses all his life.

Later Vicky went to have a look at Pebblecat. He had quietened now, and whickered as he put his ungroomed head over the door and took an apple from her hand. She breathed gently on him, and he blew sweet-smelling breath down upon her hands. This friendly approach had made them friends long ago. She spent the next half-hour grooming him until he shone.

"Morning, Vicky," said a deep voice behind her, and she turned to see two men approaching across the stable yard. One man was a stranger, of medium height and thick-set. The other was the Guv'nor, small, slim, an ex-jockey who still rode sometimes, his keen, brown face beaming down at Susan, who skipped around the yard for a while, and then wandered away.

"Open up," said the Guv'nor, and Vicky, with a smile, reached for Pebblecat's halter, opened the door, and at a nod from the Guv'nor led the horse out. Pebblecat stepped daintily out and stood quite still.

"Take his rug off," commanded the Guv'nor's gruff voice, and Vicky pulled off the navy blue rug with the horse's name on it, and saw the stranger's eyes light with admiration at the glossy coat under-neath. She stood at the horse's head while they looked him over.

"I'll try him," said the stranger, "with your per-mission."

Mr Conway's face was expressionless as he nodded to Vicky to saddle up. He helped with the bridle, and Pebblecat began to stamp restlessly. No sooner was the stranger in the saddle than he bucked, leapt, and did his best to unseat him. Vicky looked at Mr Conway in alarm, but he only smiled and nodded.

"Mr Williams will manage him," he assured her.

And Mr Williams did. He took Pebblecat round the park, tried him at the jumps, which he mostly refused and had to do again, and even forced him over the water jump at the third attempt. Mr Con-way frowned.

"Better do his box while he's out," he told Vicky.

Never had she seen a horse box in such a mess, straw trampled and tossed about. She reached for a broom and rake, took the refuse away and fetched fresh straw. She spent the next hour making Pebblecat's bed. Round the edges she left the neatly plaited straw.

Mick came back before she had done. "You sure deserve a prize for that bed," he told her. "Never in all me born days did I see anythin' like it." Vicky was beginning to know Mick. Praise often meant something up his sleeve.

"Mick," she faltered, "what are you doing with Pebblecat?"

"Now that's what I didn't want to tell ye," admitted Mick, "but if ye must know, the owner's instructions are to sell him or shoot him." Vicky's eyes filled with tears. "How many times have I told ye not to get too fond of a horse," he scolded, and stamped away, blowing his nose.

Mr Williams returned and dismounted. He and the Guv'nor began to bargain. "He has possibilities," admitted Mr Williams, "but he's difficult." (You don't know how difficult, thought Vicky.) "I'll take him off your hands . . ."

Vicky felt she would rather he was shot than go to a stranger. She thought about Black Beauty and Ginger, and what their lives had been after they left their first homes. If only *she* could buy him . . . but that was impossible.

"It's a bargain," she heard the Guv'nor's voice say, and the two men shook hands. "Come into the house and we'll settle it."

Vicky stood stroking the horse's nose. The lads were coming back for the afternoon's work, and began cleaning tack in the harness room. "Get up, me girl," Mick told her. "You wanted the chance to ride him, you'd better take it now, while he's tired. I'll go with you."

He gave her a leg up and walked beside her, down onto the beach. At the sight of the waves the horse began to quiver. "I wonder why he doesn't like the water," said Vicky.

"A wave knocked him over one day," replied

Mick. "Paddling is good for a horse, but he won't go in."

About a hundred yards from the shore was a group of rocks. Pebblecat pricked his ears and stopped. The tide was coming in fast. Vicky urged him forward, but the horse stood trembling.

"Better take him along the edge," advised Mick. Then: "What's that?" as there was a thin cry from the sea.

"It's Susan," cried Mick. "Out there on the rocks. Let me have that horse."

Vicky glanced up. Crouched on the black rocks was a small figure, waving and calling to them.

But as Mick laid his hand upon him, Pebblecat started away. Vicky held on tight as he backed from the water's edge. Then, "It's now or never," she decided, "he's *got* to go in."

She urged him forward, gently, firmly, talking to him. As the water splashed his legs he champed his teeth and stopped.

"Come on, Pebblecat, another step; that's right. I won't let it hurt you." Now they were in about three inches of water. The horse's tail flicked uneasily, but Vicky had him tight by the knees and under the double bit. Forward, forward . . . now the small waves turned about his knees.

Susan called again, and his eyes rolled and his ears pricked in her direction. Then he started forward again, this time without hesitation, and soon he was belly deep in the sea, near the rocks. But

how to get near them? The waves were buffeting his chest, and Pebblecat threw up his head and neighed. There was a splashing beside them, and Mick's small figure scrambled onto the rocks. In a moment he had caught up the child and, as Vicky urged the horse nearer, a wave smacked his shoulder and he staggered. Vicky gripped hard and held the bridle tight as Mick thrust the little girl onto the saddle before her. Mick went down into the water and came up clutching the stirrup. Before the next big wave came, Vicky turned the horse and they began their journey back to the beach.

Only as Pebblecat trod the stones did they see the two men running down towards them.

"Susan," gasped her father, as he took her from Vicky's grasp.

Mr Williams took the horse's bridle and gave a hand to Mick, who was still gasping and spluttering. The whole party made for the trainer's house. Hot baths and hot drinks and dry clothes soon revived them, and Mick declared himself as good as new, and left to finish his work.

Susan, curled up in her father's arms, was soon asleep and put to bed.

Vicky went to join Mick, who was rubbing down Pebblecat, and they made him a hot mash which he much enjoyed. Perhaps this would be the last time, thought Vicky sadly.

The Guv'nor called to her as she made to leave. "I know what you feel about Pebblecat," he told her. "After what he's done I'm deeply sorry he has to go, but I've orders to sell him or. . . . But a bargain is a bargain, and I've given my word. He won't make a race horse, he's been left at the post too many times. And race horses must earn their keep or go." Vicky knew it cost a lot of money to keep a horse in training. What was to be done with him?

She made no answer.

"Mr Williams thinks he'll do well at show jumping, with firm and patient handling. He can be firm — and you can be patient. How would you like to go with him?"

"With Pebblecat?"

The Gov'nor nodded. "I shall be sorry to lose you — and you can stay here if you prefer. But if you go with Mr Williams you can have a comfortable bed-sitter in his house with another stable girl."

"Where?" asked Vicky, wondering if her parents would agree.

"Mr Williams trains for Val Glossop," said the Guv'nor, watching her.

"Val Glossop! Not *the* Val Glossop! Is *she* going to ride our Pebblecat?"

"She'll ride him," nodded the Guv'nor, "and if I know Val Glossop, so will you. She'll have you show jumping in no time."

Show jumping, and Val Glossop, and all the summer . . . and Pebblecat. Vicky went home in a dream.

MUSICAL MISBEHAVIOUR

The girls of St Aidan's High were just coming round to thinking maybe it wasn't such a terrible place after all. For the first time, they, the Middle School, were being allowed to have a Christmas Dance as well as the Sixth Formers. Indeed, theirs looked like being an altogether better affair than the Seniors', because *they* weren't having just *records*. Jen Watkins' elder brother, Michael, played guitar in a group — Mike's Machine — and he and the other boys had offered to perform for nothing but the practice.

"Yes, everyone's really looking forward to it," said Jen to her best friend, Barbara Standring. "Makes a world of difference, having live music. Oh, how am I going to tell the class on Monday it's all off now? With their usual brilliant sense of timing, Mike and the rest of them have decided to pack up, three weeks before the dance."

"Come on, you can't blame them," corrected Barbara. "You'd probably do the same in their position. They've lost all their three nights a week work at the Unicorn, and the Unicorn's the only teenage club in Willoughby Down. Where else is there for them to play apart from there? The odd dance, that's all. Wouldn't be worth their while staying together. Granted they could play out in the country, but they'd probably spend half the money they earned getting there and . . ."

Jen looked up from the face she'd been gloomily tracing in a pile of spilt sugar and nodded in agreement to silence her friend — she did rather go on! It was Saturday afternoon when, by long habit, the girls came into town together to look at the shops . . . change their library books . . . get the occasional item for their mothers. Now they were recovering over coffee and chocolate-coated cream cakes in The Bean.

"Anyway, what did the manager say in his letter? What reason did he give?" continued Barbara.

"Didn't."

"Ah, well, if he hasn't got a good reason, Mike can maybe have him for breach of contract, you know."

"*Mmmm* . . ."

In spite of everything, Jen had to laugh. Barbara, who changed her choice of career at least twice a term, was currently bent on becoming a solicitor and so spent all her spare time reading — though it's very doubtful whether actually *understanding* — *Basic Principles of English Law* and things like that. The whole school found her antics quite hilarious. Before this solicitor thing, it had been a private detective! No one took her seriously.

And yet it was true what she said — Mike cer-

tainly should have been given a reason. The loyal sister streak in her now truly to the fore, Jen gulped back her coffee. She'd go and find out. She'd go round and see this manager, this Mr Hill.

"Wait, I'll come with you!" insisted Barbara. "Better not go on your own. I can just picture him — nasty, fat, sour-faced creature."

As it turned out, Barbara couldn't have been more wrong: Geoff Hill was a nice, quite slim, smiling young man, though not smiling with amusement. Jen could see that he was sincerely sorry about the whole business.

"But I've been receiving these letters. By the dozen. From all over town," he explained, reaching up for a couple from a great heap on top of the filing cabinet. "There you are."

The two friends read.

13 Woodend Drive
Willoughby Down

Dear Sir
We thought we'd just write to say
that we are really fed-up with Mike's Machine.
Couldn't you have Angel's Wings to play instead
of them? Please. We'll come back to your
Club if you do.

Yours faithfully
Anne Smith and Lisa Graham

Dear Mr Hill
   Come on — let's have Angel's Wings and
get that Mike's Machine lot off.

Regards
David Slater

"So I hope you see my problem," concluded Mr
Hill. "I've got to give the people what they want —
they do after all pay for it. I didn't mention anything in my letter; I didn't want to upset the lads. I
personally think they're OK but. . ."

"And they *are* OK," echoed Jen indignantly
when she and Barbara were alone again. "Well,
you've heard them and you enjoyed them too."

"Yes. Must be something wrong, thought. I've
been thinking, Jen — Woodend Drive, where the
girls' letter came from, is not so very far from
where we live, you know. What do you say we call
on our way home and ask them what it is about
Mike's Machine they don't like, and maybe then
the boys could put it right."

"Could do. Don't suppose they'd mind telling
us."

The end-of-November darkness was beginning
to fall already and, except for the twinkling,
teatime lights, it was as black as midnight by the
time the girls arrived at the short row of houses.

"What number was it again, Barbara?"

"13."

"Are you sure — it only seems to go up to 11!"

"Quite sure."

They searched about, turning corners here and there, but right enough, there was no 13.

"We really must have got the wrong number," said Jen at last.

"I don't know," replied Barbara, very slowly. "I think there's something funny going on."

Jen didn't like the tone of her friend's voice at all. It was the same as she'd used during those terrible months — happily now long gone — when she'd had her notion about becoming a detective. She'd driven Jen half mad, looking for crimes to sort out . . . and she still tended rather to make mysteries out of quite simple events.

"Yes, well, we must go, Barbara," she announced before the other's wild imaginings began. "It's getting late — I'm starving!"

The other nodded and the two girls returned to their respective homes, Barbara still very deep in thought.

Jen was looking forward to a nice quiet evening making some sort of Christmas gift list when the phone rang. It was quite early — she had indeed barely finished eating.

"For you, Jen!" called her father.

"Hello!"

"Jen, it's me, Barbara," came an excited voice at the other end. "I've been looking in my dad's town guide and, guess what, there's no Bailey Street!"

"Pardon!"

"*Bailey Street*, you idiot. Where the other letter that man at the Unicorn showed us came from. No such place. Like no 13 Woodend Drive. Now d'you believe me something's going on?"

"You're quite sure it was Bailey Street? I didn't pay much attention to that address."

"Positive. I remember because of the court: the Old Bailey."

Well, Jen knew Barbara wouldn't get something like that mixed up. For once it looked like her friend really was onto something, and she felt her own suspicion and anger rise.

"I see. He had the letters typed out himself probably, Barbara, just in case someone like us wandered round asking questions. Must have thought we were a right couple of fools! How about us going back and finding out what this is really all about?"

"Meet you in ten minutes outside the Infants' School," affirmed Barbara. "We'll catch the 6.30 bus. Bye!"

The 6.30 bus got the girls into town for 6.40. They arrived outside the Unicorn at 6.45, just in time to see four young men climb out of a large black van parked in front and enter by a side-door.

"Yes, we'll have a sandwich before we unpack the gear," they heard one of them say. "Think we've earned it today!"

"They must be these Angel's Wings people

who're replacing Mike," said Barbara. "I wonder if they know about all . . ." Her voice trailed off and she ran over to the van. "Jen, come here!" she called a second later.

Jen rushed over to her friend — who was in the process of winding down the driver's window, which had been left slightly open, and unlocking the van door.

"Hey, you can't do that!" she warned.

"Just you look at these!" Barbara returned. "I should have guessed."

She was inside the van now and Jen joined her to examine some of the letters, envelopes clipped carefully to them, that were piled on the other front seat.

They were all addressed to the Manager, the Unicorn Club, all demanding the substitution of Mike's Machine with Angel's Wings. Same as those the Manager had shown them that afternoon in fact — which it was now quite obvious to the girls the Angel's Wings had sent themselves, to get them extra work.

"They've done it very well, mind," commented Barbara. "All in different styles of writing, on different types of stationery."

"But wouldn't the manager find out when he answered them that there were no such addresses?"

"No, they've arranged it so he'd receive so many that he wouldn't bother replying. What now?"

Before the girls could finally decide they were disturbed by the sound of two youths returning to the van, presumably to start unpacking. Jen and Barbara couldn't possibly escape without being seen, and certainly there was nowhere for them to hide inside — the van being so full of equipment.

"'Ere, what are you two up to?" a tall, very uncouth-looking character asked them, placing himself menacingly in front of the open van door so as to block it.

"Doesn't matter," muttered a second, peering over the other's shoulder. "They know now what *we've* been up to, that's what's important."

Silence followed. Probably only a minute or two, but to the terrified captives it seemed like their whole lifetimes multiplied by about ten.

"Yeah," the first replied at last, very slowly. "So what we gonna do with 'em, Reg?"

It was all too much for Jen. She remembered in an awful flash all the old films she'd seen on television in which the young heroines found themselves in similar situations . . . how she'd sat before the fire and laughed herself silly. Of course, many things seem funny — till they happen to you.

She fainted, and when she opened her eyes again the two young men were lying flat on the ground. Mr Hill — the manager — his secretary and Barbara were bending over her.

"My judo!" explained Barbara, indicating the two bodies.

"Really? You did that, Barbara?"

"Went to evening classes when I was going into the private investigator business," she elaborated. "Got to learn how to defend yourself in that game. Didn't tell anyone at school 'cos you'd all have laughed — just like you do at my law textbooks now."

Remarkable! Jen had to admit to herself that Barbara wasn't quite the impractical scatterbrain she was reputed to be, after all!

They helped Jen into Mr Hill's office, from where he phoned Mike to tell him that his group had been re-instated and to ask him to pick up the girls — he'd be too busy with the police to run them home himself.

"You were great, Barbara!" praised Jen as they waited. "Really. You know, I can understand myself because he's my brother, but why did *you* go to all this trouble for Mike?"

Just then, the door opened and Mike dashed in. He bent down and gave Barbara a quick, grateful kiss on the cheek. The blush that spread all over Barbara's face and remained there the rest of the night answered Jen's question easily!

"I believe you rather like my brother, Barbara," she teased the next day.

"Nonsense!" snapped Barbara. "I did it for the school — for the dance — that's all."

But her face was slowly, steadily, turning quite red as a plum once again.

THE AMERICAN GIRL

It wasn't every day that such an interesting new girl came to Crawford High. Clara Jones and her little bunch of friends — all mad on swimming, of course — made the new girl as welcome as they could. And that was easy, because Marina Lasky was determined to make herself right at home!

"It's not the same as I've been used to," she said on her second day in her loud American accent. "Still, while Daddy's over here on business, I suppose I'll just have to make do. Our house over here is so small! And no pool!"

Secretly, Clara was beginning to find Marina a little tiring. "Did you have a pool in the States then?" she asked politely.

"Absolutely! I can swim like a fish!" Marina replied with enthusiasm.

Clara bit back a sharp retort. It wasn't Marina's fault that she had been born with such advantages. Clara thought of her own love of swimming, and how she had to use the local overcrowded baths during the school holidays.

"We've got quite a decent pool here at school," she said. What she didn't tell Marina was that she was the school swimming champion, and proud of the fact.

"Yes?" answered the American girl lazily. "Well, I'll have to try it sometime!"

Clara was at swimming practice as usual that night, getting ready to swim for the Inter-Schools Cup later in the term. She was quite confident, having won the cup the year before. Once in the water, she built up her speed and lost herself completely in the joy of swimming.

Until a voice nearby called: "Race you, Clara!" And she was conscious of Marina streaking through the water ahead of her like lightning. Marina was an ace swimmer! It was hopeless trying to keep up. At last she stopped and trod water until Marina swept back. "I won!" she cried happily, and Clara clasped the side of the pool.

The swimming instructor, Miss Derwent, came hurrying up. "Where did you learn to swim like that, Marina?" she asked in disbelief.

Marina shrugged. "Just practice!"

"Well, with two swimmers like you two, we're sure to win the cup," Miss Derwent said. "As of now you are part of the team, Marina!"

For the rest of the session Clara trained hard, trying to keep away from Marina and Miss Derwent's enthusiasm. She felt depressed and angry. She was no longer the 'star' of the swimming team; Marina was.

"How great!" Marina was towelling her hair dry in the changing rooms when Clara came in. "Told you I was good, didn't I? And with me in the team, we'll win the cup easy!"

For that remark, she earned some sharp looks from the others in the team, but Clara only smiled politely. "Of course," she said, and turned away.

As the term wore on, Marina slowly lost her attraction and became steadily more and more disliked. She was good at just about everything and liked to remind the girls about it. And she made sure that she displaced Clara as head of the swimming team. Now it was Marina who was chosen, as most promising swimmer, to enter in the solo races, not Clara. It meant Clara had lost all hope of winning the solo Inter-Schools Cup for the second time. Her disappointment was intense, but hidden.

The day of the competition dawned and everyone seemed nervous, except Marina. They travelled to neighbouring Bradshaw High and got changed, waiting for the events to begin. And it was then that someone noticed that Marina had disappeared. Miss Derwent was worried, then annoyed. She looked everywhere, but Marina was nowhere to be found.

Clara wondered what on earth could have happened to her and thought she would just have a quick look as there was a little time before the events began. She slipped out of the school and looked down the road . . . and there was Marina, just about to step on a bus, going back to the town. Clara ran like the wind and jumped on the bus just as it moved away from the stop.

"Marina," she cried, "what on earth are you doing?"

Marina had been crying. She had a crumpled-up letter in her hand. "I got this but didn't open it until just now," she said. "My grandmother's very ill." Tears rose in her eyes. "I want to go home!"

Clara realised just how little anyone actually knew about the American girl. "But you can't go home," she said, "and anyway, we've got to swim!" She pressed the bell and when the bus slowed she pulled Marina off the bus. They began to walk back towards the school.

"I suppose you're right," Marina sighed. "But I feel so homesick. It's not what I told you at all, the truth about my life; you see, my father lost his job in the States, so he sent me over here to stay with my aunt. We weren't rich back home — very poor, in fact, and we never had a pool."

"So all those things you said — "

"Well, you all seemed to think that Americans were rich. It was good to pretend — for a while. Then everyone seemed to dislike me so much, and I became really homesick. This news about my gran was the last straw. I know you were the best swimmer before I came, Clara — well, I don't want to swim any more, please swim in my place."

"Come on," said Clara, "you're a far better swimmer than I am. You must swim." And they went back to the competition.

Watching Marina as she won the solo cup by

almost a length, Clara felt sorry for the American girl. It must have been awful to leave home that way. She decided to be much nicer to Marina from then on.

"Congratulations," she said, after the race was over. Then she took hold of Marina's arm gently. "Do you want to phone America, to see how your gran is?"

Marina's face clouded. "Yes, but my aunt isn't very well off, she doesn't have a phone — after all those stories I told you about how rich my family is! Oh, I could die!"

"Never mind about that," Clara said. "It's not far from here to my house. I'm sure my parents wouldn't mind you using our phone."

"Are you sure?" Marina looked suddenly much happier. "My gran was always so good to me — I do miss her."

Brushing aside the good wishes showered on them from the team and the supporters, the two girls made their way out of the changing rooms and into the street. At that moment neither girl really cared about the Schools Cup or even the solo cup, the issues which had once caused so much animosity between them. They didn't even stop as Miss Derwent approached. "Disappearing again?" she asked. "Anyway, well done!"

"Is this your home?" asked Marina as Clara showed her inside the comfortable house in the quiet tree-lined avenue. "It's lovely!"

Clara's mother was happy to let the American girl use the phone. As it was a Saturday, Dr. Jones was out playing golf and the house was silent.

They waited until Marina had finished. She came back looking much happier. "My father told me she's only got a chill — it wasn't nearly as serious as they'd thought at first. She'll be completely well very soon! And guess what? Dad says I can come home quite soon, because he's found a job! He wrote to me, telling me all about it — it can't have reached me yet."

Mrs Jones made some coffee and they sat for a while chatting, Marina talking about life in America. Without her airs, she was a very warm, likeable girl. "Come again any time," Mrs Jones called as the two girls made their way back to the pool.

The afternoon's events were nearly over and in their part of the competition, Crawford High had done very well indeed, winning the team cup and the solo cup, as well as prizes in other races.

Clara watched Marina walk up for the solo cup — and felt glad she had been able to help. She felt no jealousy for the cup anymore, just happiness that she had made a friend.

In the weeks that followed, Marina made a completely different impression on the class. She became well-liked and popular; now that she knew she would soon be going home, she didn't need to boast. Her father had written to confirm that, three weeks after the end of term, she would be on her way back to the States.

Clara and Miss Derwent were most surprised when Marina suggested a swimming event for the end of term. It would be a kind of water ballet, she said; formation swimming, making shapes in the water. They'd never tried anything like that before, but under Marina's expert guidance, they brought off a wonderful display, which raised the roof of the school pool, and enchanted everyone. Clara was the main figure in the 'ballet' — a gesture from Marina, who stayed out of the water to advise the others.

"Thank you, Clara, for all you did," Marina said at the airport on her day of departure. "I'm glad to be going home, but I'll miss you. You are coming to stay though, aren't you?"

"Just try and stop me!" grinned Clara, already looking forward to her Easter holiday trip.

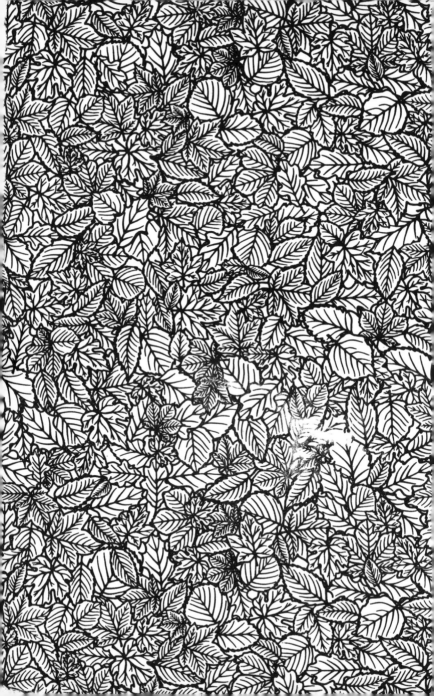